BOYS & TOYS

ACES WILD, BOOK 9

MORNINGSTAR ASHLEY

Boys & Toys

Aces Wild, Book 9

Copyright © 2019 by Morningstar Ashley

ALL RIGHTS RESERVED

This book is a work of fiction. Names, characters, places, and incidents are a product of the author's imagination or are used fictitiously. Any resemblance to actual events, locales, or persons, living or dead, is coincidental.

All products and/or band names mentioned are registered trademarks of their respective holders/companies.

Cover Art by Designs by Morningstar

Edited by Quintessential Editing and Proofreading

Proofread by Steph Marie & Anita Ford

Formatting by Flawless Touch Formatting

First Edition, November 2019

ACES WILD

Ace's Wild is a multi-author series of books that take place in the same fictional town. Each story can be read in any order. The connecting element in the Ace's Wild series is an adult store owned by Ace and Wilder. The main characters from each book will make at least one visit to Ace's Wild, where they'll buy a toy to use in their story! The only characters who crossover to each book are Ace and Wilder. And with various heat and kink levels, there's sure to be something for everyone!

CHAPTER ONE

Kalen

The Notorious Bacon Thief

KALEN WALKED OUT OF HIS ROOM AND DOWN THE HALL TOWARD THE kitchen. He was fucking tired. A late night of drinking, dancing, and loud music did that to a person. He had no regrets, though. He was young and planned to enjoy every day and night of the college experience.

It wasn't early, especially for a Sunday, but the kitchen was in chaos mode. Typical for a houseful of young college guys who were perpetually broke or too damn lazy to do more than walk to the kitchen and pour a bowl of cereal.

He walked past Dean, one of six guys who lived in the off-campus house, grabbing half the pile of bacon from his plate.

"What the fuck, man? Get your own food." Dean was the hangry type.

"It's not like you made it." As soon as Kalen had walked in the room, he'd seen his best friend Smith put the plate down in front of Dean.

Smith was the only one of them who wanted to cook, at least regularly. Kalen could, and often did, cook simple meals to get his mind off things or if he was nervous and needed an outlet. But mainly, in Kalen's mind, that was why microwaves and takeout had been invented.

Smith was always making some delicious-smelling food. Mainly for himself. But none of them were blind to the fact he always seemed, by some miracle—at least that's how Smith tried to play it off—to have extra to share with Dean. Kalen's best friend wasn't the shy type or good at being subtle. Dean would starve if someone didn't take care of him. Kalen had once seen the guy eating Taco Bell sauce out of small packets when he was broke.

"Kalen, stop being a dick and leave his food alone." Smith hadn't bothered to look away from the stove and the food he was cooking. His voice never strayed from sounding slightly amused.

"As the bestest best friend in all the world, you could make *me* some bacon."

Smith scoffed. "You buy the bacon and pay me twenty bucks, then I'll make it for you."

The other guys all chuckled. Kalen, smiling, said as sweetly as he could manage, "You don't make *Dean* pay you for your meat."

A chorus of groans and laughs went around the room. Dean deadpanned, "Oh, good one, Kalen," rolling his eyes at the same time Smith spun around, arched his eyebrow and smiled at Kalen. But it was a smile that promised retribution when Kalen would least expect.

Kalen rolled his eyes at Smith, grinned down at Dean around the piece of bacon he stuffed into his mouth, and continued his path to the Keurig that sat on the counter. Grabbing his mug, he placed it on the little platform and went about brewing his cup of coffee. While it did its thing, Kalen turned around, leaned his ass against the counter, and crossed his arms. He watched Reid and Logan chatting away over something on Logan's phone as they ate their Fruit Loops, and Dean shoveled food into his mouth. They all had gone out with Kalen the previous night.

All except Jax.

Jax was Smith's younger brother by two years and was basically allergic to people. He only lived with the five of them because their mom had asked—*told*—Smith to let Jax live with them all so he wouldn't get mummified in his dorm room from lack of social interaction. Kalen wasn't convinced being with them had helped much. Jax still never went out with them and was often in his room, far away from all their loud mouths.

But Kalen wouldn't complain either.

He'd never told his best friend, but he'd had a crush on Jax since… forever really, but it had blown up to be more than a simple crush in the last year or so. Kalen couldn't help it. The boy was fucking gorgeous—like could be a model on magazines *gorgeous*. Hence why Kalen had come up with the nickname Superstar for him.

Jax knew he was good looking, too. He didn't care and never used it to get his way or manipulate people, but he was judged by it. People always assumed he was charming and outgoing, but once they tried to talk to him, they learned Jax was anything but.

The kitchen was large with an open floor plan. The only divider was the island that split the space up. Since there were six guys living in the same house, and they often had friends over, they'd put in two tables. A small table with a few chairs sat in the far corner of the room. No one usually sat there—other than Jax—since they all gravitated more toward the bigger table that dominated the space.

Grabbing his cup—now full of caffeine and goodness—and putting a few donuts on a plate, Kalen walked over to where Jax sat alone at the smaller table in the room.

Kalen sat in the chair next to Jax, thunking his cup down on the table's surface. Jax never looked up from his phone. He'd been trying to get Jax to open up to him, but it was like pulling teeth. He wasn't even sure Jax liked him on the most basic level.

"When are you guys leaving for your trip?" Dean asked Logan and Reid. The guys were best friends and the only two who had been willing to share a room when Jax had moved in.

"The Saturday before Thanksgiving. Our drive back home is long, and we want to get there by Monday. You guys?"

"I gotta work on Saturday, so I'm leaving Saturday night right from work. I'm flying out, so I won't be missing much," Dean replied.

"Kalen and I are leaving Sunday," Smith answered for them both. "The rest of the gang are leaving Friday, but they got lucky and don't have classes Friday."

"Can't believe none of you are going home for Thanksgiving. Lucky bastards. I wish we could go on the ski trip with you." That came from

Logan. The guy had been whining about going home and missing the ski trip for weeks. Kalen got it. If the choice was between spending time skiing with friends or sitting at the kids' table at a holiday dinner, Kalen would choose the former every time. His family was great, but he was only young once, and ski trips didn't come around all that often for college kids living off their parents.

"Oh, shut it, man. You know your mom would cry her eyes out if we missed even one holiday. We've got spring break this year to go party with friends," Reid said.

"Yeah, yeah, I know."

"Jax and I only got out of going home because our parents went overseas with our sister, Mia, for some cheerleading competition."

Kalen remembered when the brothers had gotten that bit of news. Smith had been over the moon, especially since their parents had offered to pay for them to go on a trip of their own. Smith was the only one to take them up on that offer. Jax, on the other hand, had the complete opposite reaction, or non-reaction, really. He wasn't upset and whiny, but he hadn't been a happy camper about not seeing his sister for the holiday break. The siblings were all close, but Jax and Mia were the best of friends and talked multiple times a day via text and phone.

"Speaking of trips, I've got to get my ass in gear if I want to go. This damn paper Mr. Harwell gave us last week isn't going to write itself," Kalen said.

"I can't believe he gave you a research paper a week before a fucking holiday," Smith complained.

"I know, but there's nothing I can do but work my ass off to get it done." Kalen wasn't going to bitch about something he couldn't change. It wasn't worth the energy.

Jax added a nugget of knowledge to the conversation. "From what I've heard, he does it every year, always right before a break. Each year, he chooses a different break so the new students coming in don't know which one it's going to be."

It was the first thing Jax said since Kalen had walked in the room forty minutes ago. Jax never looked up from his scrolling, but at least now, Kalen knew Jax had been paying attention to them. *And maybe to me, too?*

Jax's wavy, light brown hair was long on top and typically styled in that sexy, messy bedhead way. Right now, though, it was flat and flopping down, brushing his forehead.

I wonder what he'd do if I brushed his hair back?

In the summer, instead of his hair getting lighter like his siblings' hair did, Jax's got a reddish tint to it. It was beautiful. And just one more thing that had set him apart from his brother and sister.

The Marsh kids were all attractive, but Jax stood out with his sexy good looks, his default expression always bordering on grumpy. Kalen liked that about Jax. His perceived grumpiness was cute and always made Kalen smile. Especially when he got all grumbly and his lips would turn down into an almost pout. It was truly unfair to other guys—like Kalen himself— who were good looking but nowhere near the level Jax accomplished just by waking up.

I bet he's cute when he's sleeping, too.

"Aren't I just a lucky fuck," Kalen replied.

Jax lifted his head and stared right at him, and Kalen stopped breathing. He could feel his heartbeat spike. His skin tingled with the hope of being touched. Kalen tried to smile, but he was sure it came off like he was some creepy stalker who was dreaming of having Jax's babies.

For a moment, Kalen thought he saw a twinkle of amusement in Jax's eyes. If Jax was amused, clearly Kalen looked like as much of an idiot as he felt at that moment. Because Jax didn't get amused. Not like Smith always did.

The spell was broken the moment Jax looked away, back at his phone. Kalen's body deflated…like Jax had been holding the strings that animated Kalen.

"Earth to Kalen."

Snapping his head around, Kalen saw all the other guys staring at him. Smith shook his head before he turned away.

"What?"

"Dude, we said we're heading to the library today. Do you want to tag along?" Logan asked, the grin on his face ear to ear.

Fuck. They all probably noticed the googly eyes he'd been making at Jax. Kalen turned to check on Smith. *Had he noticed, too?* Kalen couldn't tell. His ever-present smirk was firmly in place as he talked to Dean.

God, I hope he didn't see.

Kalen replied, "Yeah let me go change, and I'll head out with you guys." Grabbing his cup and plate, he walked over to the sink, rinsed it all off, dropped it into the dishwasher, and walked out of the room.

He gathered his bag, put his hat on, and taking a deep breath, shook himself out of the Jax-induced daydream.

Time to get his mind off his best friend's brother and back on the things that wouldn't get him a punch in the face.

CHAPTER TWO

Jax

Coffee, Sex Toys, and Porn, Oh My!

"No, Mia, you know you have to spend the next two weeks practicing for the competition. Your friends can wait."

"Of course, you'd say that. You hate people. I just want to have fun with my friends, Jax."

Jax walked around the art building, phone pressed to his ear, trying to talk his baby sister into being responsible while making his way through the crowd of students that littered the walkway. He needed to get to his next class. But coffee first.

Ignoring the first part of Mia's statement, Jax replied, "Your friends should understand you can't. When you get back from Australia, you can have fun with your friends."

"It's not them. It's me. I'm so tired." Jax stopped walking. He could hear it in his sister's voice. He should've caught it earlier. They talked every day, so he should've been able to hear she was stressed out.

"Mia, listen. High school is hard enough without these competitions, so if you are truly that exhausted with it all, just tell mom and dad. You know they wouldn't make you stay in it." Jax knew it in his heart. Their parents loved them and only wanted the best for them. If they didn't, they wouldn't be spending the money on an overseas trip on Thanksgiving. They were doing it to make Mia's dreams come true.

"But I will remind you," Jax continued, "last year you said the same thing, and the year before…" Mia loved competing, loved cheer, and loved the many accomplishments she'd achieved. Sometimes she just needed someone to remind her she didn't *have* to do it. It was something she *wanted* to do.

"Too true. Ugh, I think I'm getting old."

Jax laughed. Mia was always a bit of a drama queen.

"If sixteen is old, what am I at eighteen or Smith at twenty?" Jax started walking again.

"Past your prime, dear brother, past your prime." Jax could hear the smile in her voice.

"Such a sassy girl."

"You bet your ass," Mia replied, loudly.

"Mia—"

"I know. No swearing." Jax swore he could *hear* her eyes roll. "Are you sure you can't come to Australia with us? It would be so much fun with you there."

Jax had given it serious thought, but he'd gone to one of those events before, and he'd felt awful for days afterward. No one in his family truly got how crowds or being around strangers affected him. They were all extroverts who could talk to anyone, anywhere. Jax was not. Technically, he was an introvert. He didn't use that term because people assumed that meant he was shy. He wasn't shy. Jax was just extremely uncomfortable in crowds. It made his skin itch.

Fucking hard to make friends that way.

Even with her knowing all this, her asking again meant she really wanted him to go. "Sorry, sis. It's a no-go for me. But we'll see each other at winter break for a few weeks."

"I know. I'm just being needy." Mia laughed.

"Of course, you are," Jax said cheekily. "Alright, you, I gotta go to my next class and get my caffeine on the way. We'll talk later, okay?"

They said their goodbyes right about the time Jax opened the door to the building that housed a small café, the bookstore, and a student lounge for everyone to hang out or study in. It was a shortcut to the science building that Logan, one of his roommates, had told him about early on in the semester.

Thankfully, the space wasn't all that crowded, and Jax felt like he could take a deep breath.

The couches that were scattered around the space were mostly empty, but a few held some kids reading, and at least two had someone sleeping. Jax never understood how anyone could fall asleep in such a noisy place.

He stepped up to the line at the café to get his coffee and pulled out his phone. He might as well use the time standing in line to study for the test in his next class. Ten minutes later, he was brushed up on economics—as much as any person could be in that amount of time. He paid for his coffee and took it from the barista. Taking a sip, he sighed. That shit was like a drug.

"Jax!" He'd know that voice anywhere. Snapping his head around, Jax looked for Kalen. Jax was sure his brother's best friend didn't have a low volume setting on his voice, since he was always being so loud. Jax thought after all the years Kalen had been friends with Smith, he would've gotten used to the guy, but it just never happened.

Kalen wasn't a bad guy. Smith wouldn't be friends with an asshole. But he was brash and loud and all the things Jax found tedious in a person. Kalen went out to parties, concerts, the movies…basically anywhere people were going to be. And he always smiled. Jax was sure that was one of the key traits to be a serial killer or something.

Kalen was standing with a group. Logan and Reid were among the people standing altogether. Everyone else, Jax didn't know. *Great.*

Sighing, Jax walked over to Kalen. His plan was to get in and out as quickly as possible. Kalen clearly had other ideas. As soon as Jax stopped near him, Kalen pulled him into the circle of people and slung his arm around Jax's shoulders.

Jax was stunned. Kalen hadn't done this to him in nearly two years. Before that, Kalen had always been affectionate with him. As much as Jax had allowed, anyway.

At the time, Jax had liked it because no one else other than Mia was like that with him. His parents hugged him once in a while, but they weren't the overly affectionate type. Strangers tried to be all touchy-feely when they flirted with him, but he always rebuffed them. But then Kalen had stopped, and Jax had assumed it was because Jax was…well, Jax. Opposite in every way from Kalen.

"You have to help us settle a disagreement."

"Paper plates are bad for the planet so you should stop using them," Jax deadpanned.

The group went completely silent for all of a few seconds before Kalen cleared his throat, clearly trying to hold back a smile. "Thanks, but that wasn't the question." Jax didn't really want to get into whatever conversation they were all having, so he was hoping, if he was awkward enough, Kalen would release him.

Jax turned his face to look at Kalen and found Kalen's brown eyes locked on his. He could feel his warm breath brush against his cheeks and mouth. Kalen's smile grew wide.

In a low voice, dripping with heat Jax was sure was meant to be a joke, Kalen said, "What we were talking about was sex toys and porn."

Eyes still locked with Kalen's—unwilling to let anyone see how unsettled Kalen had made him with his comment—Jax replied, "I'm pretty sure there is someone else who would love to answer your question, but that person is not me." Jax reached up and grasped Kalen's hand to remove it. Before he could accomplish that though, Kalen wrapped both arms around him, his chest plastered against Jax's arm, and squeezed.

"Nope, Superstar. It must be you. We will settle for no other."

Jax rolled his eyes but otherwise showed no emotion to Kalen's performance. And it was a performance. Everything the guy did was for show.

"Don't call me that." Jax looked at Kalen out of the corner of his eye. He could feel all eyes on him, and his stomach flipped, every nerve unsettled and every instinct telling him to flee. There was a small part of him that liked the closeness he was getting from Kalen—the guy was like an octopus wrapped around him—but it couldn't overpower the rest of his instincts. Trying to grasp a way out and calm his racing thoughts, Jax spoke fast, hoping to speed this along. "Fine, ask your question, but get me off first."

The group immediately started laughing, and Kalen's eyes widened before aroused intent took over. Jax wanted to enjoy it. No one had ever looked at him like that, and it was exhilarating. But he was near capacity and everything was about to spill over. He couldn't be more humiliated about his words than he was. If he had a rewind button, this would be the top thing he'd go back and fix.

Kalen must've recognized the look on Jax's face, or maybe Jax was showing a lot more of what he was feeling than he had intended, because immediately, the flirty Kalen Jax knew was gone. Jax could see Kalen studying him before he silently released him.

Logan, who was standing on the other side of the group from Jax, took up his post as protector by ignoring Jax's fumbled sentence and said, "Sex toys and porn…yay or nay?"

Jax refused to blush. Not that his body really listened. He couldn't help how he reacted in these situations. But he could make the best of it to get out of there as fast as possible and save enough dignity to be able to face these people again.

Jax had no experience with either one. How could he answer this question? He had tried to watch porn once when he'd turned fifteen and his friend had told him about a free porn site. He'd watched all of about three minutes before shutting it off and never doing it again. There was just something so impersonal about it.

Jax tried to find a way to answer without giving away how little knowledge he had. "I guess, I just don't get the appeal. Why would you bother with it if it's not a real person, someone you care about who cares about you, too?"

The pensive look that Kalen directed his way had Jax wondering what he could be thinking about. He probably realized Jax was a fraud and had no idea what he was talking about.

Charlie, a guy Jax only knew by name because he'd been over to the house a few times, joked bitterly, "Well, we all don't look like you and get laid every night."

It wasn't the first time that assumption about him was made. He knew what he looked like, but just because he was attractive didn't mean he slept around.

Jax was at a loss as to what to say to Charlie. He wasn't good at quick retorts. That took a different type of personality than he had.

"Oh, nice, Charlie. You just called him a slut because he's gorgeous. Way to be a jackass." Kalen's words in his defense shocked him.

Kalen thinks I'm gorgeous?

Jax knew objectively he was good looking, but looks were a subjective thing, and with a personality and a social calendar like Kalen had, Jax was shocked Kalen ever gave him a second thought. There was no way he was Kalen's type.

"On that note, I gotta get to class."

Without another word to Kalen or anyone else, Jax bolted. Yeah, he was running away, but he didn't care. His thoughts were a mess, and he had more important things to worry about. Like his now cold coffee and an economics test.

Thoughts of sex and Kalen had no place in his brain.

CHAPTER THREE

Kalen
A Roll of the Sex Dice

Whites. Darks. Whites. Darks?

Kalen held up the white and dark-blue striped towel, looking between the two piles, trying to figure out where it belonged. His mom had gone over this with him. There were rules to follow. But it was like those people who got *there* and *their* backward. Kalen could never remember the rule.

He hated doing laundry, but clean underwear was a must. So, there he was on a Friday night, sorting his clothes into what he thought might be the correct piles. Or he hoped, anyway.

So much for going out.

Kalen wasn't feeling much like going out anyway. He'd gone out two…no, three times this week alone. It wasn't like he had to. None of his roommates were going out except Smith.

With it being a week before their prospective Thanksgiving trips, everyone was either working for extra cash or trying to complete last-minute assignments.

Kalen was definitely in the latter category.

Both washers in the laundry room were empty, thankfully. But it looked like one of the dryers was full. Kalen bent over, opening the dryer door to pull out the clothes inside when the door behind him opened. Standing back up again, he turned to see Jax walk in, a basketful of clothes in one hand, a book in the other.

"Oh, sorry," Jax said before turning back around. It was clear his intent was to leave Kalen alone in the laundry room. The reason they had two washers and two dryers was so they could do two loads of laundry at one time. It helped things move faster so the next person could take their turn. But Kalen didn't want Jax to walk away. Much like a few days ago when Kalen had seen Jax walking through the student lounge, coffee in hand, he called out to him. "Jax, we can both do laundry at the same time. My mom taught me how to share."

Kalen liked spending time with Jax. It was easier now that they shared a living space, but it still felt like pulling teeth, since Jax spent so much time in his room. A place Kalen had no excuse to go to.

Jax paused and eyed Kalen. Trying to act like Jax staying wasn't making his body come alive with want, Kalen turned back around and started to put his dark clothes in the washer and fill it up with soap. A moment later, he heard Jax start to do the same thing.

The room was longer than it was wide. The left side of the room mirrored the right, each having a washer and dryer on it. He understood the purpose of a washer and dryer on each side of the room. But now the set-up bothered him, because he couldn't see Jax's face with his back to him as they each did their own thing.

It was probably for the best. That way Jax couldn't catch Kalen checking him out. Because he would. It was hard not to. It had been the only thing he could do over the last two years when he'd realized he really liked Jax. Admired him from afar.

Now I sound like a sappy teenager with their first crush.

He put his other bag of dirty clothes on the floor and moved back to emptying the dryer.

Out of the corner of his eye, Kalen saw Jax putting the soap in the washer that held his clothes as Kalen absently pulled the items left behind out of the dryer.

Jax wasn't wearing anything particularly sexy. Just a simple pair of dark jeans, the cut slim and contoured to his lean muscular legs and too-sexy ass, and a faded, navy-blue t-shirt that stretched across his chest. Simple, but on Jax, lust-inducing.

Who was he kidding? Everything about Jax was lust-inducing.

Kalen pulled out another item from the dryer when he heard something hit the floor and roll. Still holding onto the towel, Kalen turned to see what had fallen. Looking at the floor, he saw a set of three dice that had rolled until they sat in between Kalen and Jax. Jax was looking down at the dice, too.

Examining them a little closer, Kalen could tell they weren't just regular dice. No, these had words on them. *Sex* dice. The kind you rolled and each one told you something different. One was for position, another was for an action, and the last was for what body part to perform the action on.

Kalen looked up at Jax, saw and heard him swallow. A faint blush creeped along his cheeks. Kalen smiled. He was just too fucking adorable.

Kalen couldn't hold back the sassy remark. "Well, doesn't that look like fun."

The dice had landed on reverse cowgirl, suck, and neck.

The blush brightened on Jax's face. He was sure he was sensing interest from Jax.

Jax looked up at him, a question clear in his eyes. But when Jax spoke, Kalen was sure it wasn't what he had really wanted to say.

"You dropped something."

Kalen laughed. "I wish, but sadly, those aren't mine."

"Kalen, we're the only two in here, and I *know* they're not mine."

"I don't know, Superstar, you seem like the kinky type to me." Kalen winked.

Jax rolled his eyes—something he seemed to love to do to Kalen. "Yeah, you know me. A regular sex-a-holic."

Kalen was enjoying this side of Jax. It was *almost* playful.

"I'm pretty sure it's Dean's, actually. The clothes I've been pulling out of the dryer are his. He probably forgot them in there."

"Dean? Sex dice?"

"I'm with you on that train of thought. Hard to imagine Dean being Mr.

Kinky." Kalen laughed. Kalen was sure Dean was more Mr. Vanilla. "I'm guessing they were a prank gift from a friend."

Jax nodded, still staring down at the dice. *Oh yeah, definitely interested.*

"Is it weird to say I wish I had been there to see his face when he'd gotten them?" Jax grinned.

Cheeky Jax was sexy as fuck.

Kalen grinned back. "Not at all. I was thinking the same thing."

Not wanting to lose the connection he seemed to have formed with Jax in the small space they shared, Kalen tried to think of something to keep the lighthearted mood going. Something fun that would maybe push Jax just a tad bit out of his self-imposed shell.

"You know, we could play a prank on Dean," Kalen suggested. Bending down, he picked up the dice, holding them in the palm of his hand.

"Us? How? Why?"

"Yeah, us. Because pranks are fun between friends. We could buy a few toys to go along with the things on the dice. Pack it all up together and give the dice back to him."

"I don't know…"

"Just a little harmless fun. Come on, Superstar, play mischief-maker with me." Kalen batted his eyelashes at Jax. "Pretty please?"

Jax eyed Kalen, his bright blue orbs flicking between Kalen's face and the dice that sat in his hand. Kalen wasn't sure it was going to work, but he kept his mouth shut, letting Jax figure it out without being pushy.

Kalen could tell the moment Jax decided to do it and grinned.

Jax sighed. "I think I'm going to regret this."

Kalen replied, "Stick with me, kid, and I'll show you the world."

Jax just raised an eyebrow at him and turned away, finishing his laundry.

Kalen, on the other hand, felt like he'd won the lottery.

CHAPTER FOUR

Jax
Mischief-Makers

JAX LOOKED AT HIMSELF IN THE MIRROR...AGAIN. TUGGING ON THE sweatshirt, annoyed with himself.

"You are stupid." Pointing at himself in the mirror like the scolding would work.

Great, now I'm talking to myself.

Jax couldn't believe he'd agreed to go to the local sex toy store with goddamn Kalen. Going with anyone would've been stupid, but with Kalen? Jax had lost his marbles.

He wasn't like Kalen. Kalen's age wasn't the only reason he was best friends with Jax's older brother. They fit like puzzle pieces. Both loved people, were always ready with a smile, and by sheer personality alone, they had a line of willing hookups.

Jax ran his fingers through his hair, thinking of maybe just telling Kalen he'd changed his mind. He had...something else to do.

Basically, sit in my room like I always do.

Nothing wrong with that, but Kalen would probably pester him or tease him about being an anti-social, anti-fun homebody. He wasn't. He liked fun, but it was just his idea of fun was the polar opposite of Kalen's.

Out of all of his roommates, he was most like Reid. The guy was quiet, stoic, and didn't go out partying. Well, he did, but he'd once told Jax it was only so Logan didn't get in trouble. Logan was a bit of a hothead.

There was a small part of Jax that wanted to do it, though. For the fun of it.

Jax scrunched up his nose at his reflection. "You can do this. Stop being ridiculous." He was eighteen and single. Virgin he may be, but he wasn't shy. It was just a store. It wasn't like Ace's Wild would be crowded.

Enough. Making sure he had his phone and wallet, Jax walked out of the room before someone caught him talking to himself and put him in a padded cell.

Jax went outside to see Kalen waiting by his car…smiling. Always fucking smiling.

"Jax!" Kalen yelled across the yard.

Jax stopped in front of him, not smiling. He wanted to, if he were being honest. It was moments like these that Kalen looked like a kid who won the biggest prize ever. It was endearing. Jax grimaced internally. He couldn't believe he was thinking of Kalen that way. But the problem Jax had was trust. Smiling felt like opening up, like showing people his true self. The part of him that loved to laugh and make dorky jokes. For some people, that worked and didn't make them edgy. For Jax, it wasn't so easy.

Ignoring the thought, he said, "Do you have to yell?"

"Yes, because I'm excited. Surprised, too."

"I said I would come," Jax grumbled.

Kalen laughed. "I know, I know, but this is *you* we're talking about."

He had a point.

Letting it go, he walked around the car to the passenger door. "Can we go now?"

Kalen unlocked the door, and they climbed in. "I have some really cool ideas of what to get for the gag gift, but I think we should look around a bit before settling."

Jax was afraid of what Kalen's ideas would be. Intrigued, but afraid.

"It's a really cool store, and the owners are great. Super easy to ask questions, if we have any."

Of course, he'd made friends with the owners. *Who doesn't he make friends with?* "How many times have you been there?"

Kalen shrugged. "Maybe a few. A guy's got needs."

The rest of the ride was done in silence, Kalen clearly knowing exactly how to get there. The building they pulled up to wasn't what Jax had expected. He thought it would be all neon and bright flashing lights, but it was a simple brick-front building with white accents and a white sign that read, Ace's Wild. Simple. Nothing sexy about it. Well…other than the handcuffs on the sign.

They both got out of the car, and Jax tucked his hands into the front pocket of his hoodie. Looking around, he didn't see anyone he knew. That would be his luck. The one time people saw him out, it would be at a goddamn adult toy store.

Kalen was practically bouncing on his feet like an excited puppy. Jax shook his head, tipping it down to hide the small smile that slipped out. *What a dork.*

Kalen opened the door for them, holding it open for Jax to walk in first. They were immediately greeted by a display filled with edible underwear.

Nothing like jumping in headfirst.

"This way." Kalen grabbed his hand, pulling him to the right, passing a wall displaying so many things, Jax's eyes didn't know where to land. There were vibrators and butt plugs and ticklers—*whatever the fuck those are*—and quite a few things Jax had no idea what they might be used for.

He must've been staring for longer than he thought, because when he twisted his face to look for Kalen, two things hit him. First, Kalen was staring at him, a smile playing along his lips and a look of affection filling his eyes. And two, Kalen was still holding his hand.

"Don't freak. They're just toys for some fun." Kalen squeezed, then slowly let go of Jax's hand. His skin tingled. Man, Kalen was wrong if he thought the thing freaking him out was the very large, thigh dildo—a legit dildo that strapped to someone's thigh—on display. No, it was holding hands with Kalen that had freaked him out.

Trying to get his thoughts back on track, Jax said, "I think I'm about to get an education."

"You came to the right place for that, boys."

Jax jumped, quickly swinging around to see who had spoken. The man standing there was about their height but with glasses and blond hair. He was smiling, and instinctively, Jax took one step closer to Kalen, their hands brushing.

"Hey, Wilder. I guess I should've expected you guys to be here. I'm starting to wonder if you guys ever go home."

The man—Wilder, according to Kalen—laughed. "Ace's Wild is home, kid."

Before Kalen could retort, a very tall, very large man stepped up behind Wilder, arms crossed and face stern. "Kalen, what did I tell you about bringing innocents into the store?"

Wilder rolled his eyes, not bothering to even glance back at the towering man. Jax noticed there was this instinctive thing, a gravity, that Ace and Wilder had. They just knew when the other was there and were pulled together, like the way the earth orbits around the sun, drawn to its warmth and light. He couldn't tell which one was the sun, but these two were a couple. He was sure of it.

"Oh, hush it, Ace. We all know you're a big softy." Wilder glanced over his shoulder, grinning up at the other man.

Jax could see what Wilder meant…the kindness in the bigger man's eyes.

Jax studied them. It was fascinating how different they were but how perfect they fit together. Wilder with his slender frame, pale-white skin, glasses, and clean-cut look, and Ace's large, intimidating frame, mahogany skin, long dreads, and muscles for miles. Jax didn't trust people, not easily, and he wouldn't go as far as to say he trusted these two, but there was just something about them that made him feel a little more at ease.

"We are mischief-makers tonight," Kalen replied gleefully, throwing his arm around Jax's shoulders.

"Of course, you are. But why are you dragging this nice, young man into your schemes?" Ace smiled and winked at Jax. He felt…seen. Like

Ace saw *him*, not the grumpy face that instinctively fell into place when he was with people.

"It's my job to bring more victims to the dark side, Ace, you know that. Like Wilder did to you."

Ace's booming laugh rang through the store, and Wilder elbowed him. "We all know I was the innocent one. Look at me! How could *I* be the bad influence?" he said, pushing his glasses up his nose.

Wilder was right, but…"It's always the innocent-looking ones who are the true bad boys," Jax added.

"Speaking from experience, Superstar?"

Jax felt his cheeks warm. There was something in the way Kalen said that—it went straight to his dick.

Wilder asked, "What mischief are you planning on this time?"

"We're actually putting together a gag gift for our roommate, Dean. We found these," Kalen said, pulling the sex dice out of his pocket and opened his palm to show the two men, "in his laundry. We want to get some toys to go with it. It's our way of teaching the lesson of making sure your pockets are empty before you wash your clothes." Kalen grinned.

They both laughed and Ace replied, "Need any help picking out some stuff?"

"Thanks. We have some ideas but want to look around, just in case something catches our eye."

It was Wilder who spoke up this time. "Oh, I just put up the display of tentacle dildos about five rows that way." Wilder pointed toward the back of the store. "You should check them out."

"That sounds fucking awesome. Thanks," Kalen said, grabbing Jax's hand for the second time that night and tugged him along. "Let's go look."

Jax looked back over his shoulder as Kalen pulled him away, and said, "Umm, thanks."

Ace and Wilder shared a look and then smiled at him before Jax was dragged around one of the aisles and could no longer see them. Kalen didn't let go of his hand until they stopped in front of a whole shelf of glass dildos, each one shaped differently. Kalen reached down and picked up one labeled: *Alien Tentacle Dildo – Gag On It.*

"You cannot be serious?"

Kalen looked up at him. "This is perfect. It's funny and kinky, all at the same time."

"When did tentacles become a thing?" Jax had no idea people had kinks that were so…*kinky*. Pointing, he added, "Or dragon dildos?"

"Since hot aliens in porn became a thing." Kalen huffed out a laugh.

"Wait, hot aliens in porn is a thing?"

Kalen dragged him around to toy after toy. Each one making Jax's face get even more red than the last. He felt like Fifty Shades of Jax would be the title of this chapter, if he ever wrote his autobiography. Who was he kidding? He'd leave this chapter out.

Even with feeling out of his element, Jax was having fun. Kalen talked endlessly. Jax saw through what he was trying to do. He wanted to make Jax feel at ease and not think. He succeeded. Kalen was funny. Jax hated to admit it, but he was. He smiled and joked over each item they picked up. Even going as far as to show Jax how to use a set of nipple suckers.

"You put the cup part over the nipple, like this, and pump. It's like those penis enlargers you see on the ads that pop up on Facebook."

"I don't know what you're doing on your computer that Facebook thinks that's what you want to see, Kalen."

"That's top secret." Kalen winked and added the nipple suckers to the basket. "Okay, I think we got enough. Let's cash out."

They paid, splitting the cost between them—Jax had insisted since it was his prank gift too—and said their goodbyes.

They made it back to the house in record time and ran to Kalen's room. Once the door shut behind them, Jax laughed. He couldn't help it. The whole thing felt like they'd robbed a bank instead of bought sex toys to tease a friend.

Jax looked over to Kalen to see his jaw on the floor. "What?"

"Uh, nothing. It's just you laughed and…" Kalen's voice trailed off.

"I laugh." The smile slipped off his face. The simple observation made him feel defensive.

"No, I know you do, but it's been a while since I've heard it, that's all. It…you know, looks good on you." Kalen turned away fussing with the bag.

Hmm, weird. Jax knew better than to think the compliment was more than what the words implied.

"I had fun, surprised as I am to admit that," Jax said.

Kalen was looking at him again, sexy smile firmly back in place. "Yeah? Me too. We should do it again."

"Buy more sex toys?" Jax teased. He'd meant it as a joke, but the heated look Kalen was sending his way was anything but funny.

"Superstar, I'm game anytime you are." Ahh, there's the flirty Kalen Jax knew so well. "But that's not what I meant. What I meant was we should hang out more."

Jax wanted that too. "We should," Jax said quietly.

And for the first time in a long time, Jax had something to look forward to.

CHAPTER FIVE

Kalen

No Tentacle Left Behind

KALEN SNUCK DOWN THE HALL AND BACK INTO HIS ROOM. JAX WAITED IN there, sitting on the floor in front of the coffee table, leaving the loveseat empty for Kalen.

Jax looked good in Kalen's room.

It had only been a couple of days since they'd gone to Ace's Wild, so the sight of Jax sitting in his room smiling still made it hard for him to breathe. Jax was always dressed in jeans and t-shirts, both on the tighter side. Another thing Kalen would not complain about.

The night he'd seen Jax laugh for the first time in years, Kalen hadn't thought it was possible for Jax to get even more good looking. But he had, and it short-circuited Kalen's brain. The man should be on billboards and magazines as a service to the world. But after spending the last two days preparing the gag gift and just hanging out, Kalen wasn't inclined to share Jax with anyone.

"Did you do it?" Jax whispered excitedly. Kalen really wanted him to stop whispering. His voice got all husky, fueling Kalen's imagination the last two nights.

I'm going to hell.

Kalen sat down on the loveseat and replied, "Yeah, he's in the shower, so he should find it soon. Now we just wait."

"This was kind of fun."

"You sound surprised." Kalen chuckled.

"I am," Jax replied, serious eyes never moving away from Kalen's. "Sneaking around, going to an adult store, *buying* things from an adult store...not my typical week."

"You smile more, too. You should come to the dark side more often. It's fun." Kalen winked.

"I'm not...it's not..." Jax was struggling to get the words out.

"I was only teasing, Jax. You don't have to do anything you don't want to do."

"I know that. It's just that it's hard for me. People think I'm shy, but really, I don't just trust people. It's easier to keep my distance. I'm not like you, Kalen, and I never will be."

Kalen had never thought Jax was shy. He never cowered away from things, he never hid, he just didn't engage. He was a wallflower. Now that he knew it was a trust issue, Kalen understood Jax a lot more. Thinking back over the years, it helped color some of Kalen's own interactions with him.

"And you shouldn't ever have to be someone you're not. I'm not trying to change or fix you, Jax. I think you're pretty cool as you are, grumpy face and all. But I wouldn't mind doing more fun things with you."

Jax stared at him like he was trying to figure out if Kalen was telling the truth or not.

"You have Smith, the guys, basically anyone else...Why would you want to hang out with me? We're nothing alike."

"Dude, I know, and I like that we're not. I like people. All kinds. What fun is life if everyone around you is just like you?" Kalen shrugged.

"But you don't really know me."

"Then let me get to know you, Jax." Kalen mirrored his position. He kept his tone serious, albeit quiet, and his eyes locked onto the bright blue eyes of one of the prettiest guys he'd ever known.

"No more kinky gag gifts, though. I'm not sure I can handle Kalen-level excitement on the regular." Jax gave Kalen a small smile, amusement dripping from every word.

"Fine, fine, but you don't know what you're missing out on. How about to—" Kalen abruptly closed his mouth when Dean walked in, trying so hard not to laugh at how red the poor guy's face was.

He stood staring between Jax and Kalen, a confused look on his face. Kalen didn't blame him. He was still a little shocked that Jax was in his room by choice. The shock didn't last long.

"What the fuck, Kalen?" Dean threw the bag of gag gifts toward Kalen. The rainbow gift bag that no longer had the bright red tissue paper sticking out the top, landed on the loveseat next to Kalen, spilling its contents.

"Hey, what did I do?" Kalen asked, trying for wide-eyed innocence. It wasn't an easy feat for him.

"Oh, don't try to play that card with me. I was here last year when you put all those suction cup dildos in Reid's bathroom shower. It's always you."

"He was in on it, too!" Kalen said, pointing at Jax who was suddenly wide-eyed for a whole other reason. *Yup, I threw him under the bus.*

"Please, Jax is too…*Jax* for that. Stop trying to place blame on someone else."

"I helped." Jax shrugged.

"Jax, man, you should stop hanging out with this one," Dean said, pointing his finger at Kalen. "He's a bad influence."

"You have to admit, you laughed, Dean. We picked some funny gifts," Jax retorted.

Kalen was definitely smiling now. Jax was calling Dean out and making his own face heat up in embarrassment at the same time. It was cute.

Dean flipped them both off, but Kalen could see the amusement in his eyes. He may be Mr. Vanilla and not a super fan of Kalen's, but he wasn't a bad guy or unable to take a joke. "Whatever. Just play jokes on someone else. You owe me, Kalen, for all my bacon you keep stealing." Then Dean walked out in a huff. Kalen laughed. He did steal a lot of his bacon.

Kalen looked at the bag that was still spilled out next to him and noticed there was something missing.

He stood and rushed to the open door and yelled, "Hey, Dean?"

"What?!" Dean stopped and turned back to face Kalen, amused annoyance clear on his face.

"Don't think I didn't notice you kept the tentacle dildo, perv!"

Kalen had never seen that shade of red on a human's face before. Dean stomped off to his room, slamming the door shut behind him.

Closing his own door, he turned to see Jax staring at the items on the loveseat. Kalen sat down, waiting to see what Jax's reaction would be.

"Oh my god, he kept the tentacle." Then they both cracked up laughing.

As the laughter faded, Jax's smile didn't. Kalen let out a sigh and relaxed against the back of the couch.

"Now I have dreams of playing a prank on Smith to get back at him for some sketchy, older-brother shit he played on me and Mia as kids."

"I would totally help you with that."

Jax laughed, and all Kalen wanted to do was keep making him laugh and smile. The desire for Jax was growing every day they spent together. The way his feelings for Jax had grown over the last two years was nothing compared to what was going on in his heart for the socially awkward guy he'd spent the last few days with.

Kalen wanted to kiss him. Kiss him on the lips and neck, suck and bite every damn inch of that gorgeous, creamy skin.

The tension in the room grew as the silence stretched. Kalen could see the moment Jax went from relaxed and open to rigid and closed off.

"I'll just go—"

"No!" Kalen blurted out, panicked that the moment they shared would be over before it really began. He just wanted more time. Maybe he could get Jax to like him, too. "I mean, you don't have to. You can stay, and we can play my PlayStation or watch a movie or devise ways to torture Smith." Kalen forced a relaxed grin. It probably looked like he had that damn tentacle dildo stuck up his ass.

"Are you sure? I mean…yeah, I'd like that." Kalen's body deflated with relief.

"Good, me too. Movie, game, or prank?" Kalen's smile that time was easy.

"Movie?" Jax looked around Kalen's room. It wasn't a huge room, but they'd lucked out that all the rooms could fit things like Kalen's loveseat along with a bed. The master bedroom that Reid and Logan shared was the largest in the house. Lucky. "Kalen, I don't see a TV."

"Ready for some magic? Climb up here." Once Jax was sitting next to him on the loveseat, Kalen leaned forward and pressed the button on the side of the coffee table that was hidden under the lip. Immediately, the center of the coffee table started to rise, and Jax gasped.

"Holy fuck, that's cool!"

It really was. His dad and uncle had purchased it for him when they'd seen he really had no place to put a TV. It was one of the best gifts he'd ever gotten.

Not better than the gift he was getting at that moment, though. The loveseat wasn't all that big, and having Jax pressed against him, shoulder to thigh, was doing things to his body. Kalen shifted in his seat, trying to adjust himself as secretly as he could.

"Right! I mean it's not a huge TV, but it's better than nothing. Now you gotta decide what we're watching." Kalen grabbed the remote from the arm of the loveseat, powering it up and finding Netflix. He opened the app on the TV.

"Umm, *Venom*?"

"Fuck, yeah. I love that movie."

And at the same time, they both said, "We are Venom," in the same voice as the actor did in the movie, then they were back to laughing again. It was one of the best nights of Kalen's life.

CHAPTER SIX

Jax

Brotherly Love

WALKING OFF CAMPUS TOWARD HOME AT THE END OF THE DAY WAS ALWAYS a good feeling. Doing that on a Friday was even better. Doing it on a Friday when his last class was canceled was like Christmas coming early.

In a week, Jax wouldn't have classes, and the house he shared with five guys would be blissfully empty and quiet. He could walk around naked all damn day, if he wanted to. He *wouldn't*, but he *could*.

He'd never been completely alone before, and he was looking forward to it.

The weather was a little colder than normal due to the cold front that settled over the area. Jax pulled the collar of his coat up to cover his neck. It hadn't been a smart choice to walk home, but he wanted the solitude after a particularly long day.

Jax also wanted to hang out with Kalen again. Not something he'd thought he would say...*ever*. But it was surprisingly easy to be around him. That might be due to the fact that Jax's assumptions about Kalen had been wrong. And his own feelings toward the guy had been wrong as well.

Jax had sat next to Kalen for hours last Sunday. Somewhere between the physical closeness they'd shared as they'd sat close on Kalen's couch and all the small things Jax had realized they shared in common, Jax had an epiphany of sorts. It'd been small but held quite the gut punch. He hadn't been annoyed by Kalen. He'd been jealous.

There was a fine line between love—or in his case, like—and hate. All the years when Kalen had come into their home, all the times he'd gone on vacations with them, and every time he walked into the kitchen they now shared, Jax bristled. He'd always thought it was because Kalen was this loud, forward, outgoing, loved-by-all-people guy. And he was still all those things, but Jax realized it wasn't annoyance or dislike he was feeling. He was fucking Hulk-green with envy.

Jax had never had an easy time socially. He didn't trust people. He didn't truly get why. It wasn't like he was afraid of some physical ramifications, like getting beat up, but it was more a fear of rejection. *A person can't be rejected if they don't reach out.*

The irony was, he'd never been rejected for who he was. Even his parents had easily accepted that he was gay. Granted, it had been easier since Smith had come out as bi two years before. But there were no past relationships that had gone bad, no bullying. It was just some fear he was born with that led to him trying to be perfect. He used to check the mirror to make sure every hair was in place, that his clothes looked good, that he smiled and was happy when people expected him to be.

It had been exhausting.

The house he'd been calling home for the last three months came into view as he rounded the corner. The plain beige house sat on a residential street at the edges of Vintage Ridge. It was a quiet neighborhood that was mostly filled with housing available to rent for students of UNC at Vintage Ridge.

There were strict rules when it came to parties and shit for anyone that lived there. A few of the guys hadn't been happy about those rules when they'd moved in the year before, but there wasn't much they could do about it. It was one of the reasons Jax had folded under his parents' decision to have him live his freshman year in off-campus housing instead of a dorm. He liked the quiet and liked how he never had to worry about some party with drunk, noisy college kids, filling up the space he was most comfortable being besides his childhood home.

Jax walked into the house to a wall of noise. The entryway to the living room was wide enough to see Reid and Logan had some show playing loudly on the TV. At the same time, Logan was also playing some kind of game on his phone, and Reid was reading. Shaking his head, Jax walked on toward the hall that had three of the five bedrooms.

He saw Kalen's door ajar and knocked, hoping maybe he'd want to hang out. But when the door swung open, Jax realized the room was empty. Glancing down the hall, he could see the bathroom door was also open, so he knew Kalen wasn't in there.

Of course, it was still early, so maybe he was still in class. Jax went to his own room, dumped his bag on his bed, and went back out to the kitchen. He normally ate lunch on campus, but seeing as he was out early, he'd have to make do with something at the house.

Searching for something to eat led to some frozen quesadillas he was sure he bought months ago and some soda he was sure was Smith's. Popping the top of the soda, he gulped down half the can before pulling out a pan to cook the quesadillas.

He wouldn't call this cooking, but even the simple task of heating up precooked food in a pan usually went horribly wrong for him. Putting the spatula under the quesadilla, he lifted it up to check if it was even browning like the package said it should when Smith walked in.

"What are you doing, idiot?" Smith grabbed the spatula from Jax and went about flipping the quesadillas and turning up the heat on the stove.

"I was doing just fine you know."

"No, you weren't. You had the heat too low. You would've been here forever at this rate." Smith looked over his shoulder at him and pointed to the can of soda sitting on the table. "And I never said I'd share my drinks with you."

"You're my brother. You have no choice."

Smith scoffed. "Brother or not, I bought it for me. You should've asked."

Smith was such a stickler for those things. Jax wouldn't be surprised if he had a spreadsheet on his computer that tracked his food and drinks to make sure no one else took them.

"I could always tell Mom you aren't sharing with me." Jax knew it was a low blow. According to their mom, she didn't have a favorite—really, they all knew it was Mia—but she worried the most about Jax. It was insulting, but Jax learned a long time ago to take advantage of it.

"Low, bro, low." Smith laughed, used to Jax's threats by now. Jax smiled. It wasn't like his brother would take away the drink. He was both stingy and generous to a fault. But only to those he cared about.

"I'm going out with some guys tonight to a poker game. You wanna come along? It's a small group."

Jax was lucky he was close to both his siblings. Smith had always tried to include him since they were only two years apart in age, even when he knew Jax would always say no.

"Thanks, man, but I'm just going to hang out at home."

Smith looked at him, a slightly pitying look in his eyes. Jax sighed. "I'm fine, Smith. I *like* hanging out at home."

Smith didn't reply, but Jax knew his brother. He was thinking, processing it. Smith still didn't get it, even after all these years, but at least he tried. "Maybe we should do a poker night at home with just us guys. We can use your movie collection as money." Smith winked at him as he put the quesadillas on a plate and put them in front of Jax.

Jax laughed loudly as Reid and Logan walked into the kitchen. Immediately, the laughter in him died and the normal nerves took over. Ignoring the weird looks on their faces, Jax picked up his food and started to eat.

"Uh oh, Smith. You've gone and broken the kid." Logan squinted his eyes at Jax. "Or is he drunk? I don't think I've ever seen him drunk…or laugh before."

Reid slapped Logan upside the head as he walked by him, pushing into the room and walking over to the fridge. Jax actually thought of Reid as a friend. They had a few things in common, and his calming nature was easy for Jax to be around.

"Stop being an ass. He laughs, you idiot."

Logan grumbled like he always did when his best friend called him out. "It's just not normal for Jax. And stop hitting me."

Logan sat next to Jax at the table and held up his hand for a fist bump. Jax gave in and fist bumped the idiot. He was a good idiot but still an idiot. Logan was lucky to have Reid to keep him out of trouble.

By the time Jax was halfway through his food, Smith had finished cooking his own lunch, and Reid and Logan had heated up pizza from the fridge and sat down with Jax.

They didn't often eat together, and Jax could admit to himself that it was nice to at least eat with his brother.

"Are you guys still going to Red's poker game tonight?" Smith asked. Red was a friend Smith had met a couple of months after starting at UNC. Her name wasn't actually Red, but Emily. Everyone called her Red because of the color of her hair.

Reid and Loan both nodded. "We're going over early to help her set up the food. It's Logan's way of paying her back for breaking the lamp the last time we were there."

"Which is stupid because I offered to pay for the damn thing, but she said no." Logan often sounded like a petulant child when he spoke. Jax would never understand why Reid was friends with the guy.

Smith laughed. "She's trying to teach the unteachable a lesson. Poor girl."

Reid laughed when Logan flipped Smith off and went back to stuffing his mouth with pizza.

"Where's Kalen? I thought he had an early day today, too?" Reid asked.

Jax tried not to act more engrossed in their conversation than he was before. He didn't want to give away his interest in all things Kalen to any one of them. They'd never let him live it down.

Smith replied, "He did. He went over earlier than planned since Red's brother flirted his way into getting Kalen to do what he wanted." He waggled his eyebrows, obviously driving the point home since anyone who knew Kalen would know what Smith's statement meant.

The sour feeling in Jax's stomach pissed him off. He shouldn't care that Kalen was off flirting with someone else. That was Kalen. Jax was under no illusion that Kalen was his or ever would be. Kalen would never be able to settle for someone like Jax. There were just too many differences that would keep them apart.

Smith nudged him and asked, "Are you sure you don't want to go tonight? It'll be fun."

For a minute, Jax thought about it. He could go and show Kalen that he was more than an introverted homebody. But the idea of going, even for Kalen, held no appeal. He smiled at Smith and shook his head. "Thanks for the invite, though."

Smith watched him as he got up and put his plate in the dishwasher and left the room. For some reason, Jax had a feeling Smith knew why Jax wasn't as happy as he had been when he'd walked into the kitchen.

Jax sighed. There was nothing he could do to change that. Nothing he could do to change himself either. Closing his bedroom door behind him, Jax flopped onto his bed and stared at the ceiling. He never felt alone, but at that moment, he felt more alone than ever.

CHAPTER SEVEN

Kalen
The Most Elaborate Murder Plot

It was dark out by the time Kalen walked into the house. All the lights were off, and the completely quiet house felt eerie. Being a Friday, he wasn't surprised it was so quiet, but he wasn't normally home to enjoy it.

He walked into the kitchen, grabbing a bottle of water out of the fridge, and then went back out toward his room. Kalen looked down the hall at Jax's door and saw the light shining out from under it. Kalen paused, staring at his door then back at Jax's. He knew Jax would still be awake since it was still fairly early for a Friday night.

Pushing open the door to his room, he dropped his bag on the bed and walked back out, water bottle still in hand. The worst thing that could happen is Jax could turn him away. But he had a need to see Jax, to talk to him and make him laugh. It'd been a rough day. He had planned to come home after his last class early that morning but got roped into helping move some stuff around in the science lab for one of his professors—the price of being a nice guy to everyone—and then cornered by Red's twin brother, Jason—who everyone but Kalen called Blue for his blue eyes—to help with the poker night set-up. A poker night Kalen had never wanted to go to.

Normally, he would go and hang out and watch them all play but it'd been a few days since he got to talk to Jax, and he wanted to just be near him more than anything. Kalen was afraid if he waited too long this opportunity to be with Jax would pass him by. Then he'd lose out on being with a guy as special as he knew Jax was.

Still being quiet, he walked down the hall, took a deep breath—because, of course, this is when he'd get an attack of nerves—then knocked. He heard a yelp and something thumped on the floor inside the room, and he had to hold back a laugh. Clearly Kalen had startled Jax.

"Who is it?"

"It's me, Superstar."

"I can hear you laughing."

Kalen loved how affronted Jax often sounded when he was talking to him. Like every tease was unwarranted and beneath his station in life.

"Noooo, I wouldn't do that. Not to you." Kalen covered his mouth with his hand, trying not to let any sound escape.

"Whatever. Are you coming in, or are you going to spend the rest of the night pestering me through the door?" Kalen shook his head. Jax thought no one could hear the amusement in his voice when he was acting all affronted, but after years of hearing him speak to his siblings, Kalen could hear it clear as a bell.

"I don't know. This seems like fun. We could play a game—" Jax pulled the door open before Kalen finished his sentence, and what do ya know, Jax was smiling.

"Asshole." Jax stepped back, leaving the door open for Kalen to come in.

The room was the same size as Kalen's, but where Kalen's was navy blue and white and not at all decorated—he was a college student with no sense of style at all—Jax's room was all gray tones with dark-purple and sky-blue accents and decorative shit on the walls and nearly every surface. Kalen could tell he'd taken the time to make the place feel like a space Jax wanted to be in, and he'd succeeded.

"I'm a little jealous, Superstar. My room looks like a dump compared to this." Kalen walked in and looked around. Jax didn't have a loveseat like Kalen did, but he had a bigger bed, a small desk that sat in the corner of his room, and a large dresser that sat opposite the end of his bed with a large TV on it.

"It's just a room. No better or worse than yours." Jax's face was pink. How endearing for him to be embarrassed about his room when, really, he should be showing it off with pride.

"Sure, and the Eiffel Tower is just a tower with pretty lights." The comment made Jax laugh and Kalen smiled. One goal of the night achieved.

Kalen didn't know where to sit and didn't want to assume Jax would be okay with him sitting on his bed. It felt intimate to sit where Jax slept.

He walked around the room looking at the more personal touches Jax had clearly put a lot of thought into. The first thing he saw was a picture of all three of the Marsh siblings on Jax's small desk in the corner of the room. Kalen recognized the picture.

"I remember this. This was about six years ago, right? At that camp your parents used to make you all go to every summer for family vacation."

"Yeah, I remember Smith had tricked you into going by telling you all these great things we would be doing."

Kalen turned back around, leaned against the desk, arms crossed over his chest, and smiled. "That was the trip I stopped believing everything your brother told me."

"I could've warned you about that long before that trip." Jax chuckled, as he leaned back against the headboard of his bed, long legs stretched out in front of him.

"I still can't believe we made crafts with so much macaroni I couldn't stand to even look at it for weeks." Kalen's mom had been happy about it, but Kalen had missed eating one of his favorite foods.

"Yeah, the Marshes sure know how to liven up a vacation."

"Oh, and your mom's cooking! I'm certain that traumatized me, and I'm sure it's a crime against the camping gods that there was no place to go swimming."

"Oh god, my mom's cooking! That was always the worst part for me.

She would never let my dad help, either, not that he was much better."

Kalen laughed. "Sure, he was. He could order takeout with the best of them."

"True, and he still can."

Awkward silence took the place of laughter and shared memories. Kalen didn't know what to do which was a first for him in social situations. He always knew what to say. But this was Jax, and somehow getting the guy to want to be near him and want to date him was making Kalen's brain short circuit.

"Kalen, you're being weird, and it's freaking me out. You can sit on my bed."

Kalen's face heated up. Jax had called him out. He wasn't wrong. Kalen wasn't going to admit being with Jax made him feel like he wasn't as experienced with guys as he was.

He went to the bed, sat down facing Jax, and crossed his legs. This close to him, Kalen could smell his cologne. Jax always smelled so fucking good. He wanted to bury his nose in Jax's neck and draw the scent of him into his body and hold it there.

There was another bit of silence, this one not as awkward as the last. He took the time to study Jax, who was fiddling with his phone, and realized how much Kalen hadn't known him before this. It continued to shock Kalen, what with Jax being so open with him now, but he should've realized earlier it wasn't that Jax was changing. It was that Jax was growing more comfortable, more trusting of Kalen. That had something close to pride filling him.

"Can I ask why you're not at the party still?" Jax's question was quiet, his eyes locked on his phone screen, and Kalen got the impression the answer was somehow important to Jax.

"I wasn't going to go in the first place. I mean, I don't really play poker, but Jason cornered me when I was helping one of my professors today and wouldn't take no for an answer."

Jax looked up at that, confusion on his face. "Why weren't you going to go? You love going to those things."

"Yeah, but not always." Kalen had been learning to say no. Not often, because he did love people, but he was a junior in college, and his classes had been getting harder and needed more of his attention. He wouldn't be a college student forever. "When it comes to Red's parties, I don't mind saying no. Her brother annoys me."

"I've met Blue. He seemed nice. *Loud*"—Jax chuckled—"but then, most people are."

"He isn't a bad guy. Just the clingy type, which is not for me."

Jax nodded, staring at his phone screen again before locking it and throwing it on his nightstand. "You guys hooked up then?" Jax was looking right at Kalen.

His voice was steady but quiet. "No. But not for his lack of trying, though."

"You ever have a friend-with-benefits relationship before?" Jax asked.

Kalen was confused by the change in subject and hesitantly answered, "If you're asking about Blue, no."

"Not Blue, just in general." Jax sat forward. His face close enough that Kalen could reach out and pull him the last few inches and kiss him, if he were brave enough.

"I did once. It was back in high school."

Jax opened his mouth to ask, but Kalen cut him off. "And no, it wasn't your brother."

"Eww, that was *not* what I was going to say." Jax threw a small bed pillow at him and Kalen laughed.

"I know, but I couldn't help it." Kalen threw the pillow back at Jax. "How about you?"

Jax's eyes widened. "How…how about me what?"

Kalen tilted his head, questioning what he was seeing. "Have you ever had a friend-with-benefits relationship?"

Jax audibly swallowed. His fingers started to pull at the pillow in his lap. Kalen waited. He wasn't going to push.

"Honestly, no. But then, I haven't…What I mean is I've never…"
Never?

There is no way Jax was saying what Kalen thought he was saying. Jax was his Superstar. Gorgeous and smart and sexy. There was no way that…

"I haven't had sex before."

Never had sex. Jax had never had sex. Kalen's dick twitched. He closed his eyes, trying not to get turned on by that. His cock did not listen.

Jesus. Why is that so hot?

"You've never...?" Kalen's voice squeaked. He coughed and tried again. "You're a virgin?"

Jax sighed but looked at Kalen, his bright blues eyes holding a little embarrassment. "Yeah, v-card holder since 2001," Jax joked.

Kalen reached out, putting his hand over Jax's fingers that were still pulling at the pillow. "First, don't be embarrassed by that. There's nothing wrong with it."

Jax scoffed. "Right, because guys love to hear that the guy they want to sleep with is a virgin and has no idea what he's doing." Jax shook his head before he continued, "You know most guys don't even believe me because of my face? How fucked up is that?"

"Well, those guys are assholes and can fuck off. They don't deserve you, Jax." Kalen paused. Not believing what he was going to say next. In for a penny and all that. "I think it's hot as fuck. Maybe you just need to find the right guy." Kalen shrugged, trying for nonchalance and feeling like he might come out of his skin for that admission.

Jax was once again wide-eyed, staring at Kalen. It was becoming a pattern. "You think a guy being a virgin is hot?"

Kalen immediately shook his head. "No, Jax. I think *you* being a virgin is hot as fuck. Not just some guy."

"Oh."

Kalen locked eyes with Jax. He wanted him to see the certainty in his eyes. The air around them was heated, like the furnace had been turned up. Kalen didn't know what to do to tone things down. He wanted Jax too much, and his admission had opened the floodgates to his feelings and desires.

Before he could come up with something to say, Jax moved quick, pressing their lips together. Kalen was stunned, shocked, flabbergasted. Any and all words could not describe how he was feeling at that moment. Then he felt Jax's tongue run along the length of his lip as he moaned, and Kalen was gone. Done. He couldn't hold back. Kalen opened his mouth to Jax. Using his right hand, Kalen grasped Jax's neck, pulling him closer.

Jax climbed onto Kalen's lap, knees straddling Kalen's thighs, their chests pressed together. Kalen was in fucking heaven. He wanted to pinch himself to make sure he wasn't dreaming, but he couldn't manage to remove his hands from Jax's body. Didn't *want* to remove his hands from Jax's body. One still held onto Jax's neck as they kissed. The other was busy roaming Jax's back and ass.

He felt Jax's fingers tugging at his shirt, and Kalen obeyed. Lifting his arms, he let Jax take his shirt off, and a moment later, Jax's fingers were caressing every inch of Kalen's exposed skin. Their breathing was heavy as Kalen stared at the sight of Jax in his lap, now playing with Kalen's nipples and eyes locked on his naked torso like he was mesmerized by it.

But there was something he needed too. "Off. Take yours off, too." Kalen grabbed the bottom of Jax's t-shirt and pulled up. Jax's fingers moved away from his skin giving him a moment of clarity, a moment he could've stopped what they were doing but he didn't. Jax was an adult. Virgin or not, he knew his own mind, and apparently, he wanted Kalen.

As soon as the shirt flew through the air to land somewhere on the floor, Jax was back to torturing Kalen's skin with his soft touch. Kalen moaned, loud. Then he kissed Jax again. Needing Jax's taste on his tongue, Kalen drove his tongue into Jax's mouth and devoured him. Not once did their hands stop exploring all the naked flesh that had been exposed.

They were frantic. Kalen felt like they were speeding down a highway in a convertible, the top down, the wind making it hard to breathe. It was perfect, and he wanted more.

"I need…more." It was like Jax had ripped the thought from Kalen's own head. He'd thought it, and Jax said it. Then Jax was moving back, dragging Kalen onto his knees. They kneeled there on Jax's bed, face to face, both breathing like they'd run a marathon, staring into each other's eyes. Kalen smiled. He couldn't help it. Jax was…more than words could describe. Kalen was wrecked in a way that made him think all his fantasies were coming to life.

He reached out, slowing the moment down for just a minute, and ran his fingers through Jax's hair. Soft. So, *fucking* soft. Kalen wanted so badly to tug on it and run his fingers through it as Jax wrapped his lips around his cock. To feel it on his thighs when Jax sucked his balls and licked his rim. Just everything.

I want it all with him.

Jax whimpered. The sound going straight to Kalen's balls. He tugged Jax back in, sealing their mouths together again. He needed more contact, wanted that intimate connection with him.

In no time, Jax was frantic again. He began pulling at Kalen's jeans. Kalen returned the favor, pulling at Jax's. Before long, their jeans were open, and their hard cocks were out.

Naked. The *goddamn* man was going commando.

"I swear this is one elaborate murder plot."

Jax pushed back, his face scrunched up in confusion. "What did you say?"

"I think you're trying to kill me," Kalen said as Jax stared at him. "You have no underwear on. I'm only human."

Jax smiled. "No killing. We haven't finished yet." Jax leaned in and kissed him, deep and hard, before pulling back and winking. *Legit winking.* "But maybe later."

Who is this guy?

Kalen laughed. How could he not? Jax was adorable, even while sexed out. Kalen reached out, wrapping his hand around Jax's dick.

Nothing had ever felt so goddamn good.

But he was wrong, because the moment Jax wrapped his hand around Kalen's cock, he almost shot. "Oh god."

It was everything. Jax was everything. Kalen was sure he'd never been so turned on in his life.

They both knew what to do. Kalen moved his hand first, stroking ever so slowly up then down. They had no lube, but when he removed his hand so he could use his saliva, Jax grabbed it with his own, uncertainty and heat written all over his face. "What...why did you stop?" Jax asked breathlessly.

"We need lube."

Jax's brows furrowed for a moment before understanding hit him. He bent at the waist, reaching toward his nightstand. Kalen stopped, his eyes traveling down the length of Jax's body, pausing on his ass. His perfectly biteable, naked ass. Jax's jeans, loose from being unbuttoned and unzipped, were pulled low. Kalen bit his lip. Jax's ass was right there.

Kalen heard a snick that drew his gaze away from Jax's ass. He had pulled out a bottle of lube and was pouring some into his own hand. Kalen, not wanting to be left out, put his hand out. Afterward, Jax tossed the bottle next to them on the bed and wrapped his slick hand around Kalen's hard cock, pulling a moan from him. Jax's hand on him was indescribable.

Wanting Jax to feel what he was feeling, Kalen wrapped his hand around Jax's shaft. Kalen pulled Jax to him with his free hand and kissed him. Their strokes were fast, bordering on painful, but Kalen loved it. With the slight burn from the speed, Kalen's dick was getting more and more sensitive to Jax's touch. He felt the tingling in his balls and knew he wouldn't last much longer.

"Gonna come."

Those simple words coming out of Jax's mouth sent him higher.

"Me too. Oh, god, me too."

The burning ache in his balls was building. Kalen could feel Jax trembling in his arms. Jax's cock throbbed in Kalen's hand.

"Oh fuck…"

"That's it, Jax. Show me. Want to see you…"

Jax whimpered, his grip tightening on Kalen's dick. That whimper… god. It was over for Kalen. The pressure that had been building released in blinding pleasure and white ropes. Kalen squeezed his eyes tight as the intense pleasure of his orgasm wrecked him. Then he felt it. Felt Jax's release and opened his eyes not wanting to miss it.

He's beautiful.

Their hands slowed then stopped. Jax looked blissed out and done. Kalen reached down, grabbing Jax's shirt that hadn't gone flying as far as Kalen's had, and used it to wipe their hands and stomachs.

Once he had them both clean, Kalen gently pushed Jax until he was lying down on his side. Kalen tossed the shirt and mirrored his position.

Jax smiled at him. A new sort of smile. It was content and sweet, and Kalen wanted to stay like this forever, just staring at him.

"I thought you didn't like me." The honest words slipped out of Kalen's mouth.

Jax just continued to smile. "I guess you were wrong."

Kalen had never been happier to be wrong in his life.

CHAPTER EIGHT

Jax

Awkward Mornings

JAX WOKE UP TO THE SUN SHINING THROUGH HIS CURTAINS. OBVIOUSLY, with everything that had happened, he'd forgotten to close them. Sighing, he stayed there, lying on the bed, staring at the ceiling.

The night before had been hot. Jax had thought about it, had wanted it over the last week as he'd gotten to know Kalen better, but never truly thought it would lead to one of the hottest nights Jax had ever experienced.

Coming from a virgin, that wasn't saying much, though.

Jax looked around the room, noticing all the signs that Kalen had been in his room the night before. Doing more than just talking. Jax grinned at the thought.

He was happy Kalen hadn't tried to spend the night in his room. Jax was sure the morning after was going to be hard enough without having to wake up to the guy lying in his bed. Not to mention having to sneak Kalen out of his room without any of their roommates seeing him. Namely, Jax's brother.

Not something Jax was ready to face.

As comfortable as he was, the rumbling of his stomach and his about-to-burst bladder were getting hard to ignore. Climbing out of bed, Jax pulled a t-shirt on he had laid over the back of his desk chair and padded down the hall to the bathroom to empty said bladder.

Stepping back out of the bathroom, Jax walked down the hall toward the kitchen. As soon as Jax entered the room, he stopped. His eyes locked on the sleep-tousled Kalen frying bacon across the room. He felt his face flush. Kalen's back was to him, but watching him move about while cooking, the night before flashed through Jax's mind.

There was nothing sexual about what he was doing, but the movement of the muscles in his arm and the sway of his hips reminded Jax of Kalen's arm when he was stroking Jax off and how his hips moved with every stroke of Jax's hand on Kalen's cock. He felt a noise bubbling up from inside himself, but thankfully, before it could escape, he heard a loud cough, breaking him out of his fantasy.

Looking toward the main table in the room, Jax saw it was filled with all of his roommates. Reid was looking down at his phone, but the rest of the guys were staring at him.

"What?" His brother smirked. Jax glared at him.

"Not a word," Jax said, pointing his finger at Smith.

"Morning, Superstar." Kalen's bright, cheery greeting brought Jax's focus back to the man who had been in his bed.

"Hey."

Oh good, if the hot night didn't snag him, my powers of speech sure will. Jax was mentally face-palming.

Ignoring the looks from his nosy-ass roommates, Jax moved over to the counter to fix his own breakfast. The bacon and eggs Kalen was cooking smelled good, but Jax refused to ask him to cook him some. He didn't need that witnessed by the Nosy Nancies in the room.

Walking around Kalen, Jax lightly brushed against him when Kalen had unexpectedly stepped in Jax's path. He whispered a quiet, "Sorry," to Kalen and got a smile in return. If Jax wasn't mistaken, Kalen's face was tinged with a look of embarrassment.

Jax returned the smile and then grabbed his mug from the hook on the wall, putting it on the Keurig, and started his coffee. He took a deep breath to try and calm the sudden butterflies in his stomach. Then Jax walked over to the fridge and bent over, pulling the freezer drawer open, grabbing his sausage, egg, and cheese sandwich. He stood back up, planning on using his leg to push the drawer closed, but instead, Jax bumped into a solid wall. Hands on his hips clued Jax in to whom was behind him. His breath caught when Kalen's voice, low and slightly husky, spoke directly next to his ear.

"Sorry, didn't mean to bump into you." His hands squeezed once then were gone.

Jesus fuck.

Making breakfast had never been so fucking hot before. Jax was sure someone had raised the temperature in the room, because he could feel the sweat rolling down his back.

Jax put his sandwich in the microwave to heat up and stood there as it went round and round on the glass turntable. He tried not to look at Kalen, but no matter how many times he criticized himself for doing it, his eyes would once again find Kalen's.

Once the microwave beeped, he took the sandwich out then reached up into the cabinet for a plate and set it down on the counter. He took the sandwich out of the paper towel it was wrapped in and dumped it on the plate. Grabbing the plate, Jax turned to walk across the room to sit at the table.

But the world was out to get him or embarrass him as much as possible, because at the same time he stepped back to turn, Kalen stepped to do the same thing. They collided, Jax nearly dropping his plate as he tripped over Kalen's foot. But Kalen caught him, grabbing his arms and pulling him close. They stood there chest to chest, eyes locked on each other. The moment felt like forever.

"What the fuck is going on with you two? Did you hook up?" Logan asked, his voice loud in the suddenly quiet room.

All too quickly the moment was over because of their rude-as-fuck roommate, and Jax suddenly wished he lived alone.

"Shut up, Logan," Reid said, followed by the required smack upside the head.

Kalen smiled at Jax, released his arms, and turned to look at their roommates but directed the reply to Logan, his smile still in place. "You seem awfully interested in Jax's sex life, Logan. Tsk, tsk, tsk. Smith will have to kick your ass."

"Why are you volunteering me for shit? You kick his ass," Smith grumbled.

"And ruin my pretty face? No, thank you."

Jax smiled and rolled his eyes. "Don't everyone jump to defend my virtue."

Everyone but Logan laughed.

"Thanks for saving my food," Jax said to Kalen, who nodded in response.

Jax went over, placed his plate on the table then, making sure Kalen wasn't right behind him, went back and grabbed his coffee. Sitting down at the table, Jax gulped down some of the, thankfully, still-warm coffee and took a bite of his sandwich. When he looked up, all of the guys were staring at him.

"What the fuck, guys?"

"Umm, why are you sitting here?" Dean asked.

Jax felt the focus of their stares right to his core, but the words hurt more. It made him feel unwanted. He knew he normally sat at the other table when they were all there, but he didn't deserve to be called out for it. Going to stand up to move back to his normal table, he was stopped once again.

"Sit down, Jax."

The look on his brother's face was the one he often used on him as a kid. It meant there was no use arguing because he was going to get his way no matter what. Jax sat back down.

A moment later, Kalen was at the table, sitting in the seat next to him. Under the table, Kalen squeezed his leg but didn't leave his hand there. Jax's cheeks definitely flamed red that time, but Jax looked at him and smiled. He knew Kalen was telling him he was there for him, and Jax appreciated that more than Kalen could know.

"Oh. I get it," Reid said.

Jax looked over at Reid, and his face was as calm as ever as he looked right at Jax and Kalen.

Logan replied, "See? I was right."

"It's too early to follow your weird half-conversations," Jax said, going back to drinking his coffee and eating his food, but not before he saw that same knowing—but not exactly happy—look he'd seen before on his brother's face.

Jax hated that Smith knew him so well.

He pointed at Smith again. "Don't make me tell Mia on you."

Smith scoffed but looked away. Jax took a deep breath and let it out.

Kalen laughed at something on his phone while he ate. It was always the simple things that affected Jax the most. They shouldn't have made Jax's heart squeeze, but they did.

He was so gone. Jax was sure it was too soon, but he wouldn't walk away. He wanted Kalen. He just had to figure out how to keep him.

Kalen
More Things Bind Us, Than Separate Us

KALEN WALKED room to room looking for Smith, needing to have a conversation with him.

He wasn't looking forward to the questions the conversation was going to cause, but Kalen was also sure he was making the right choice. He thought about it, and really, the answer came easy.

Finding Smith in Dean's room wasn't a surprise. They often spent time together, Smith helping Dean with his schoolwork. Kalen was sure there was more to it than that, but Smith was a very secretive and protective person when it came to Dean. Kalen wasn't surprised because the little he knew about Dean led him to believe he needed a little protection and support. Maybe it was completely innocent, but Kalen was hoping it was more. Smith needed someone to love.

Standing in the door, Kalen waited quietly to draw Smith's attention until Smith was done pointing and directing Dean to do something on his computer. Smith stood up as Dean typed and clicked on different things. Smith, still supervising.

"Hey, man. You got a minute?"

Smith looked over and nodded, squeezing Dean's shoulder before he walked toward Kalen. They ended up in the backyard. It was November in North Carolina, so it wasn't exactly warm, but they both had hoodies on.

"What's up?"

"I wanted to let you know I can't go on the ski trip anymore."

"What? Why the fuck not? It's been planned for weeks."

Enter questions Kalen had wanted to avoid but knew he couldn't—and the guilt of bailing on his best friend.

"I know, but you know that project Mr. Harwell gave me last minute? It's still not done, and it's not looking good." It was a small fib. The project wasn't done, but that's only because he'd been spending a lot of time with Jax…or thinking about Jax…or dreaming about Jax.

"Fuck. What are you going to tell the guys?" Smith asked.

Valid question. There was a group of them—Dean being the only other roommate included—all going in on the expenses together, and if Kalen didn't go the assumption was his part of the cost wouldn't be there either.

"I'll still pay my part for the house and the beer." Kalen laughed. "I'm sorry, man. This is just too important." Kalen really meant it too, but the real reason he was staying behind was to spend time with Jax. Things were finally falling into place with them, and Kalen wanted to keep things going in the right direction. What better time than when the house was empty of nosy roommates, and Jax could relax without worrying they would be watched or caught?

Smith nodded but didn't look very happy. Kalen got it. It wasn't all the time they got to go on these types of trips.

"Alright, but just don't turn into my brother while we're gone. I don't need two people who hate leaving the house." Smith smiled and Kalen relaxed, knowing his best friend may not like Kalen not going, but he wasn't mad either.

Kalen punched Smith on the arm, and they walked back into the house. Smith went back to Dean's room, closing the door that time, and Kalen walked down the hall and knocked on Jax's door.

He'd stayed in his room after breakfast that morning. Kalen didn't blame him really. They'd been less than subtle around each other. Good thing the house would be empty within the next couple of days.

"Come in," Jax's muffled voice said from inside.

Kalen walked in, closing the door behind him. Jax was sitting on his bed, laptop on his legs.

"I'd ask if you're watching porn but then I remember that's not like you." Kalen laughed.

"Ha, ha. I'm watching a movie on Netflix."

"Oh fun, whatcha watching? You better not be watching anything stupid like Arsenio Hall or *Zombieland*."

Jax gasped. "First, who the fuck is Arsenio Hall? Second, you cannot come in my room and knock *Zombieland*, dude. That is not okay."

Kalen groaned and put his hands over his face. "You like *Zombieland*? I don't think I can hang out with someone who likes that movie." Kalen peeked out between his fingers and saw the smile on Jax's face. Score one for the day. Kalen smiled back, dropping his hands.

"Funny man," Jax said, before looking down at the computer in his lap and back up at Kalen. "You…want to stay and watch something?"

Kalen nodded and walked over to Jax's bed. He sat down next to him, pressing his body close to Jax. Kalen wanted to make sure Jax knew he wanted more than a simple friendship with him.

Jax moved the laptop so it was on both of their legs, and Kalen glanced at the screen and noticed he was watching one of Kalen's favorite movies, *Extinction*.

"Fucking fantastic movie, Superstar."

"It's one of my favorites."

Kalen stared at Jax. They were opposite in so many ways, but Kalen was learning they truly shared so many things in common.

Not being able to help himself, Kalen reached out and pulled Jax the rest of the way and kissed him. A simple press of lips. Chaste compared to the kisses they'd shared the night before. But Kalen wanted this to show Jax a part of what he was feeling.

When they separated, Jax smiled at him. Kalen cleared his throat, looking away from Jax, afraid of what his reaction might be, and said, "I'm not going on the trip next week."

"What?" Jax whispered the words.

Kalen didn't say anything for a moment, then he looked up at Jax, unable to help himself, and continued, "I'm staying here. With you. I just told Smith I couldn't go because of my paper which is true but mainly… it's to spend time with you. I hope…I hope you're not disappointed."

Happiness shone in Jax's eyes, before his mouth lifted in a smile. "No. Not at all." Then Jax kissed him, fast and sweet. "Let's watch the movie."

CHAPTER NINE

Jax

Kalen Gets a Little "Knotty"

JAX HAD BEEN IN HIS ROOM FOR HALF THE DAY WHEN HE SUDDENLY HAD the urge to go sit in the living room. When the guys were home, he was always in his room—no complaints about that—but now that they were gone, the idea of sitting out there and not being bothered by shouting or the blaring TV sounded awesome. Add in curling up on the couch and Jax was sold.

Not having a loveseat or comfy chair was the one thing he sometimes regretted about getting a bigger bed. It meant always having to sit on his bed or desk chair. Not always the most comfortable of seats.

Grabbing his book, Jax left his room and settled in the living room on one of the couches. Pulling the throw blanket that was draped over the back of the couch, Jax covered his lap to ward off the chill the cooler November month brought, and began reading again.

The room was quiet, and the sofa so comfortable that he, once again, found himself lost in the book until he heard a car pull into the driveway.

Kalen had left that morning, claiming he had some errands to run. Jax got it. He often ordered the things he needed online to lower the amount of times he had to go out to the store. Which mostly had to do with hating shopping rather than not liking people. He could be lazy with the best of them.

He heard the door open then close and a rustle of bags.

"Did you bring back food?" Jax yelled out. He was a little hungry and a lot lazy, so getting up again and rummaging the kitchen for food held no appeal.

The only response he got was a laugh. Jax rolled his eyes, smiling.

Weird guy.

Kalen walked into the room, bags in hand, and Jax immediately knew what Kalen had bought was not food.

"Oh, god, you didn't!"

"I did, Superstar, I did. But have no fear, you will love what I got."

"That's debatable."

Kalen dropped the bag on the coffee table and sat next to Jax on the couch. "Would I ever steer you wrong?"

"Yes, and I'm sure if I asked anyone, they would agree that you are a bad influence on little ole, innocent me." Jax fluttered his eyelashes playfully. Kalen barked out a laugh.

"Yeah that's because they don't know you and your pervert heart. Don't forget, I know you went to an adult store."

Jax gasped. "Dude, you brought me there!" Jax reached over and punched Kalen's arm. Kalen fell back in mock pain, crying about abuse. Jax smacked him with one of the throw pillows, making Kalen laugh. "Jackass."

Kalen sat back up, wiping his eyes. "You know it, baby." Winking at Jax, he pulled the bag he'd placed on the low table onto the seat cushion next to him, blocking Jax's view from whatever was in it. "Now let me show you what I got."

Jax saw Kalen's arms moving and the rustle of the bag as he pulled out the first item. Kalen turned back around to face Jax but left his hands behind his back.

"Don't get the wrong idea from the package. These are not edible," Kalen said in a mock stern voice, one that teachers often used, but with a glint of humor in his eyes. Bringing it forward, Kalen handed it to Jax.

Reluctantly, Jax held out his hand to take it. It was a small box. As soon as Jax read the box he laughed, tears falling down his cheeks.

Bacon Condoms. Make your meat, look like meat. Lubricated with bacon lube.

Through the laughter, Jax said, "I cannot believe you found this."

Kalen replied, "I'm sure that's not true."

Taking a deep breath, Jax tried to calm down before replying, "You're probably right. But now I'm afraid of what else you have in that bag."

Kalen reached in, once again turning his back to Jax to hide what he was pulling out. Facing Jax again, Kalen said, "Close your eyes."

Jax shook his head, finding it impossible not to smile. "Nope, not happening."

Kalen laughed again. "Oh, come on. It's not that bad. I promise it's nothing squirmy or alive."

"That leaves out a whole host of things, Kalen."

"True, Superstar. You just gotta trust me, I guess."

I do trust you.

It felt like everything stopped. The fact that thought came on instinct, no decision on Jax's part, was huge. Because Kalen was right, he had to trust him. The best but scariest part was he did trust him.

Smiling, Jax said, "Alright, hand it over." Then he closed his eyes and held out his hands. There was a long pause. Jax knew the significance of what he was doing, acknowledging his trust in Kalen by simply doing exactly what he'd asked Jax to do, was not lost on Kalen either.

Then something was in his hands. The package was hard and felt like plastic. He squeezed his fingers around it, trying to figure out the shape of it. After the bacon condoms, Jax knew whatever it was couldn't be worse than the list of things his crazy brain was telling him it might be.

"Open those pretty eyes, Jax."

Jax opened his eyes and looked down at the thing in his hands then cocked his head to the side in confusion. "There is no way this is what it looks like."

Kalen chuckled. "If you think it's a couple of dildos shaped like veggies, then you'd be right."

Jax looked up at Kalen. "But…" Then back down at the…vegetables and back up at the guy. "Why? Don't get me wrong, they're funny in an odd Kalen kind of way, but vegetables?"

The grin that graced Kalen's plump lips was warning enough for Jax. Some kind of innuendo was about to come out of Kalen's mouth.

"I just thought you could use some veggies in that body of yours."

"Oh, you did. You said it." Once again, Jax found himself laughing with Kalen. He realized he'd never had more fun with any one person than he was having that night with Kalen. The man's sense of humor was skewed somewhat to the crazy end of things, but it suited him so well.

"Well, at least they're vegetables I like." Jax winked.

"Oh, he makes jokes!" Kalen exclaimed. Then the process repeated itself, and within a few minutes, Jax was sitting, eyes closed, hands out, trying to figure out what was in the next hard plastic package that was in his hands.

"This better not be that orca whale penis dildo thing we saw in Ace's Wild. I won't be so forgiving for that."

Kalen barked out a laugh. "Like I would buy that."

Kalen's tone was what Jax would call sarcastic outrage.

"Suuuuure," Jax replied.

"Well, go on and look."

Jax opened his eyes, looked down, and wanted to laugh…again. "Oh my god, it's…it's a metal butt plug."

"Not just any butt plug, though." Kalen paused for dramatic effect. Then continuing in a whisper, he said, "This one is *magic*."

Jax rolled his eyes playfully. *Dork.* "Yes, I can see that. What completes any butt plug is a Magic Eight Ball base, of course." Jax laughed and shook his head.

"I see you are smart, young one. You will go far if you use this tool for good."

Line after line that came out of his mouth, Kalen made him laugh. It felt good.

Then Jax held his hands out, eyes closed, without having to be asked to do it. But this time, Kalen was quiet. No jokes or laughs. Jax lifted one lid, sneaking a peek at Kalen to see what he was doing. But what he saw wasn't what he'd expected.

Kalen looked nervous.

Jax continued to watch him. The games were fun but it was more important to make sure Kalen was okay. As Jax watched, Kalen took a deep breath and let it out.

"Everything alright? You're not trying to scare me with that strap-on for your thigh thing are you?"

Jax heard a small laugh come out of Kalen. He relaxed a little and waited since he knew if he could make Kalen laugh it wasn't something too bad.

Kalen placed something in his hands. Squeezing around it like he had with all the others, Jax felt softness. It surprised him a bit since all the others were packaged.

"Okay, you can open your eyes."

Jax heard the apprehension and nervousness in Kalen's voice and became nervous by extension. Jax opened his eyes and saw what looked like some kind of soft rope in his hands.

"I know this isn't like the others. I just figured…I guess since you've never used these things that you could with me. I mean use them." Kalen rushed on to add, "Not that you have to. I know what you said before, so I thought…hoped that if you wanted to, I could show you what it's like to use these things with someone who cares about you."

Jax's brain was on overload. He couldn't pinpoint which thought he should focus on. Was it the rope and soft cuffs in his hands and all they implied? Was it the offer to use them and all the other things with Kalen? Or was it the fact that very subtly—like covert-ninja-spy subtle—Kalen just said he cared about Jax?

"You want to tie me up?" Jax's voice squeaked. No one could blame him.

Kalen's eyes got wide, and his mouth dropped open, before suddenly Kalen grabbed and tossed the rope and things onto the coffee table, and pulled both of Jax's hands into his own.

"No, no that is *not* what I meant. I mean, that's hot but that's—" Jax found himself once again with his head cocked and absolutely confused. "I meant you could…you know…tie *me* up and use the toys on *me*." Kalen said the words quietly but with such confidence Jax was sure he'd given it a lot of thought.

"Jesus, Kalen. You want *me* to tie *you* up?" The trust Kalen was giving him was beyond words.

"Absolutely. I find it kind of hot." Kalen shrugged and gave a small laugh.

Jax leaned forward, placing his forehead to Kalen's and closed his eyes. "No one's…That's not an offer I would refuse, but Kalen? I don't know what I'm doing."

Kalen nodded gently. "I know, and I can help direct and guide you."

Jax sat back and replied, "And I find that kind of hot," making Kalen laugh.

Kalen pushed their mouths together. It started off soft, just lips against lips. Then Kalen's tongue was teasing between Jax's lips. He felt alive like he had electricity coursing through his every nerve. All Jax could think was more, more, more.

Kalen moaned, the sound reverberating through him as Kalen slowly eased Jax backward, until he lay on the couch. Feeling the weight of someone, of *Kalen*, on top of him made Jax feel undone and out of control. Jax loved it. Every sensation was more than he ever imagined it would be.

Kalen settled between his legs. Jax felt the hard ridge of Kalen's erection press onto his own. His body, reacting on its own, thrust. The action rubbing their jean-covered cocks together.

"God that feels so good, Jax."

"It does. I just…I just don't know what I'm doing here."

"Just keep doing what you're doing. I've got you."

Jax had no idea being with someone would feel like this. So fucking alive. Like he would burst at any moment.

They rutted against each other as they kissed, feeding each other their moans. Jax didn't want to stop, but he felt too close and it was too soon. He wanted this to last longer, to experience more with Kalen.

"Too much, Kalen."

Kalen slowed but didn't stop. "Good?"

Jax nodded. "Too good. We need to stop, or it'll be over before it begins." Jax chuckled. A smile pulled at Kalen's lips, his eyes never leaving Jax's.

Kalen did stop and sat up slowly until he was on his knees on the couch, grabbing Jax's hand on the way. Jax looked up—Kalen kneeling in front of him, his messy hair, his flushed cheeks—and Jax just wanted to forget what he'd said and pull him back down on top of him.

"You should stop looking at me like that, or I'll end up doing what your eyes are begging for."

Jax whispered, "Would that be so bad?"

Kalen reached out and ran his fingers down Jax's cheek then back up and into his hair, tugging on the strands. Jax moaned, and the laugh Kalen let out sounded evil and dirty.

"Never bad, but we can make it better. Let's go to your room where you can have your wicked way with me."

Kalen stood and pulled Jax up with him. He gathered all the things he'd purchased and tugged Jax down the hall to his room.

Jax wasn't going to lie to himself. He was nervous as fuck but so turned on it didn't matter. He had Kalen there with him, to help Jax make it good for them both.

When they entered Jax's room, Kalen threw the bag of stuff on the end of his bed and then reached back and pulled his shirt off over his head. Kalen was beautiful.

They hadn't taken anything off since they were together last time. Getting to see Kalen's pale skin, wanting to touch it, already made this the most intimate thing Jax had ever done.

"You alright there, Jax?"

Jax knew Kalen was asking if he still wanted to go further, and he did, no question.

Jax replied, "Hell yeah. I'm good. But…you could take your pants off." Then Jax grinned, not being able to hold it back.

His balls ached and his cock was throbbing, reminding him with every heartbeat what his body wanted, but his mind was so lost on this guy. Jax just wanted to make Kalen feel good, tease him, and make him smile.

Kalen stepped toward him as he unbuttoned his jeans. "Anything else?"

Jax swallowed, trying to wet his suddenly dry throat. *Talk about being hot.*

Kalen's pants dropped to the floor and he stepped out of them, leaving them where they fell, never taking his eyes off Jax. Jax couldn't help himself. Who could with all that soft skin in front of them, tempting them? Kalen was sexy as fuck. From his dusty-rose-colored nipples, to the trail of hair that traveled down his belly into his black boxer briefs, to the swell that was hidden by the fabric.

"Jax? You with me?" Jax looked up, and Kalen's eyes locked on his with a hint of humor in them. Jax had the urge to stick his tongue out at him but refrained. It wasn't his fault the guy had so much sex appeal.

"Yeah, the underwear. Can you..."—Jax gestured with his hand at Kalen's boxer briefs—"remove them?"

"Are you going to tie me to the bed while you're completely dressed and I'm at your mercy all naked and vulnerable?"

Jesus Fuck.

Jax closed his eyes tightly and reached down, squeezing his cock to help stave off his orgasm.

"You play fucking dirty." Jax wasn't equipped for how hot an aroused, *focused* Kalen could be.

Kalen laughed. "You like it. But I'll play nice. Only because I want you to come *on me* and not in your underwear."

Jax groaned.

Kalen walked away, over to the side of the bed, before bending over to remove his boxer briefs. Kalen's naked ass was right in front of Jax, his hole exposed for the briefest moment before Kalen stood and crawled onto the bed.

The guy had confidence in spades. As Kalen sat there, cock hard and standing straight up from his body, he emptied the bag at the end of the bed and unwound the rope. Kalen paused in his task, looking up at Jax.

"Naked. I want to see you naked."

Snapping out it, Jax did what Kalen said, removing his shirt then pants but pausing at his underwear, suddenly nervous to remove that last piece of clothing.

Stalling, he picked up their clothes and stacked them neatly on the dresser that held his TV. When he turned back around, Kalen had the rope undone and the cuffs secured around his wrists.

"You are so goddamn beautiful."

Kalen's cheeks flushed, and Jax felt like he won the fucking lottery. A sudden sense of rightness took over, and Jax used that to boost his confidence, pulling down his underwear and tossing them to the side.

Kalen's eyes roamed his body. It felt like a physical caress to Jax.

"Come tie me up."

Jax went to the bed, and by the time he got there and stared down at Kalen, Kalen was laying down, holding out the rope for Jax. He took it, studied it, tried to figure out how to do it.

"Jax, look at me."

He did and was caught by the gentle look Kalen was giving him.

Holding up his hands, wrists together, Kalen said, "You see the D-rings on the cuffs? Thread the rope through them until you have enough to tie it around a couple of the bars of your headboard."

Jax found the end of the rope and did just that. Once Jax thought he had enough, he stepped closer to the bed which pulled Kalen's arms above his head.

Looking around, he couldn't figure out how to tie him to the headboard without shoving his junk in Kalen's face. And for some reason that felt kind of...rude. Which Jax also knew was ridiculous since that was the whole point of being naked with a guy—to get up close and personal with their junk.

He attempted a few different ways to do it, but none seemed to accomplish what Jax wanted. He'd been so focused on how to maneuver himself he *sort of* forgot about Kalen until Kalen laughed.

"I see what you're trying to do, but I won't be upset if your dick gets up close and personal with my mouth."

Jax huffed but felt his cheeks turn pink. Because of course.

Jax knelt on the bed by Kalen's head, trying very hard—no pun intended—to ignore the fact he could feel Kalen's breath on his dick. As he pulled the rope around to tie it, the end of the rope hit Kalen in the face.

"Oh shit, sorry."

Kalen laughed. "No worries. Just keep going."

Jax did, but the rope just kept hitting Kalen over and over. It was maybe down to his lack of knowledge in rope tying—a sailor, he was not—or his utter clumsiness. Who knew?

Not to mention his dick slapping against Kalen's face, numerous times. Jax was convinced Kalen was to blame since he kept making excuses as to why he had to move, which *always* happened—like Jax believed it was oh so innocent—to be closer to Jax.

By the time the rope was secured the right way, with much guidance from Kalen, Kalen had little pink marks from the rope on his face, and they both were laughing hard.

"I think we failed at this," Jax said.

Kalen turned his head, looking right at Jax and replied, "Shh." Kalen pushed toward Jax, pursing his lips, and Jax indulged him. Kalen kissed him with a sweetness he didn't think was possible. "It's okay…better than okay, to laugh and have fun during sex. And I am having fun, Jax." Then Kalen kissed his nose.

Jax grinned and nodded to show his understanding.

"What now then, almighty teacher?" he teased.

"So sarcastic. Grab the lube from your drawer, then climb up on the bed and sit between my legs."

Jax followed Kalen's instructions. He looked up at the man stretched out in front of him and wanted to touch every part of him, kiss and lick and bite.

Kalen bent his legs and spread them wide, and Jax felt the breath leave his body. Every moment of this experience was more than he'd ever had and still not enough.

"Lube your finger," Kalen instructed in a husky voice that sent tingles down Jax's spine.

Jax picked the bottle up from the bed. Opening the cap, Jax poured some on his finger.

"Now fuck me with it, Jax."

Fuck.

Kalen cried out when Jax pushed a finger inside him. Jax stilled and stared at where he was. A part of him was inside of Kalen. He shivered and took a deep breath. He fucked Kalen with his finger, listening to him moan and pant. With every thrust, Jax could feel Kalen's hole relax, and when he thought he should put another one in, he looked up at Kalen to make sure.

"Can you take more, Kalen?"

Kalen nodded, frantic. "Yes, more, please."

Jax pulled back then pushed in with two fingers. With every moan and groan, with every thrust inside the tight heat, Jax grew more confident in what he was doing. On the next push in, Jax curled his fingers and rubbed Kalen's prostate, making Kalen buck his hips and push back against his hand for more.

Jax felt like he was flying.

"The plug, Jax. Put the plug in me." Kalen's broken words snapped Jax out of the trance-like state. Looking up, Jax saw a Kalen he had never seen before. His face flushed red and sweating, his pupils blown wide with need, his thighs pulled back toward his chest, opening himself up to Jax's view, and his prick hard and leaking all over his abs. Jax wanted to see him like that again. Just for Jax.

Jax picked up the plug and laughed softly at the Magic Eight Ball on the base. Only Kalen would get something like that. As Jax moved the plug to put lube on it, the little triangle inside the ball moved. Jax laughed at what it predicted.

"Kalen, guess the Magic Eight Ball is truly magic."

Kalen looked up, and Jax tried not to laugh too hard and shake the plug as Kalen read the words out loud.

"This butt's for you." Kalen barked out a laugh and Jax joined in.

When the laughter died out, they were both there staring at each other, and Jax felt the need to kiss Kalen. Kneeling up, Jax leaned over Kalen's prone body and kissed his lips, his flushed cheeks, then down his neck and collarbone, nipping at his nipples as he went lower with each kiss. Finally, Kalen's hard leaking cock was right in front of Jax, and he didn't think twice, just leaned down and swiped at the pre-come with his tongue and moaned at his taste. Jax wanted another taste, but he knew if he did, that the plan of fucking Kalen with the plug would never happen. Jax sat up and reached for the lube, ignoring the whimper that came from Kalen.

Jax poured lube onto the plug, dropped the bottle, and then slathered the slick all over, coating every part of it.

"Jax, babe, it's good. Just please put the thing inside me. I need…"

Jax caressed Kalen's inner thigh. "I've got you." Kalen smiled.

"Push it in slowly."

The end of the plug had bumps. They started out small, went wide then back to small again. Over and over, as Jax pushed, Kalen's rim resisted until it gave in and sucked in each ridge. "Oh fuck," Kalen rushed out with each ridge that popped in. "Just like that. Keep going."

When the plug finally bottomed out, Jax was panting and Kalen was moaning.

Jax started with shallow thrusts. Slow and steady to drive Kalen crazy. Then before Jax knew it, Kalen was fucking himself back on the plug when Jax pulled each ridge of the plug out then pushed it all the way back in again.

"Jax, stroke…me."

Jax reached out and wrapped his hand around Kalen's cock, flushed purple, the skin tight and hot to the touch. With every fuck of the plug and stroke of his hand, Kalen seemed to get more lost in his own pleasure. Jax wanted to jerk himself so badly it hurt, but he wanted to continue to drive Kalen crazy even more.

He squeezed Kalen's cock tighter, stroked faster, and felt the moment Kalen was going to go over the edge. Jax thought about stopping, prolonging the moment, but the need to see Kalen release was stronger. He felt Kalen go rigid, his cock spasming and shooting his release up over Jax's hand and his own chest and abs.

"Come on me, Jax. Do it now."

Kalen was squirming all over, but Jax released his cock and, using Kalen's come as lube, stroked himself. Jax whimpered, not being able to hold in any sounds that fell from his lips. Kneeling up between Kalen's thighs, he watched Kalen watching him, seeing his want and need for Jax to come on him. Jax's balls drew up tight, and he felt his body go hot and shake as everything but Kalen fell away.

Jax came, calling out Kalen's name.

He gave himself a moment to recover before getting up to pull out the plug and uncuff Kalen's hands. They didn't speak as they cleaned up, and they lay down together on Jax's bed, Kalen pulling Jax to him, entwining their legs, and squeezing him close.

"I've never felt anything like that," Jax admitted.

"Me either, Jax."

Jax's heart soared.

CHAPTER TEN

Kalen
Crushing Confessions

"Nooo, I don't want to move." Jax's voice was muffled from being buried in Kalen's neck. He'd fallen asleep as they'd watched yet another movie.

"We have to eat, Jax. I can hear your belly, and I'm sure if you died of starvation, Smith might kill me."

Jax grumbled unintelligible words then pushed up away from Kalen and off the bed. They were both dressed in sleep pants and t-shirts. After waking up that morning, they'd both decided they deserved a veg day.

Kalen wished every day could be this way. They hadn't slept in the same bed yet, but waking up and having Jax all to himself made him feel things he didn't think were possible two weeks ago.

It was Wednesday, and Kalen felt like their time alone was going by too fast. He wanted to cherish every moment with Jax, knowing it might not last more than the week they had.

They hadn't had a conversation about what they were to each other, but Kalen knew he wanted more than just a fuck buddy. Jax could never be that for him. All he knew was, before the guys were home again, Kalen needed to find a way to bring up the subject of feelings.

Jax turned back, eyeing Kalen lying on the bed staring up at him.

"Come on, lazy bones. Let's go cook, and by cook, I mean heat up some yummy food in the microwave."

They both walked down the hall to the kitchen, then heated up chicken quesadillas Jax had bought from the freezer section. They ate and made small talk then, in short order, were back in Jax's bed, the TV turned on and the blankets cocooning them together.

Kalen watched Jax, as Jax was sucked into the movie paying Kalen no mind. He still wanted to pinch himself sometimes that he got to be the lucky guy Jax trusted and wanted to be with.

"I can feel you staring at me," Jax deadpanned.

Kalen chuckled. "Can't help it, Superstar. You're pretty."

Jax looked over at him, smiling. "What are you thinking about? It was the gears turning that gave you away."

Kalen decided to be blunt and honest. "Did you know I've always had a crush on you?"

The look of surprise and confusion on Jax's face answered the question for Kalen.

"Don't look so surprised. You're a catch."

"But…me? We're opposite in every way."

Rolling on his side, Kalen gestured for Jax to do them same. Once the TV was off, faces inches apart, Kalen answered his question.

"Do you remember when we were younger, I think Smith and I were about ten, and I had come over to hang out with your brother? We were playing some video game in the game room at your house, and you were in your room with Mia." Kalen had thought of the smaller moments in his memories of Jax over the last week or so, and he saw each one in a new light.

Kalen continued, "I was getting bored, but Smith didn't want to do anything else. I remember getting up to go see what you guys were doing, but you were no longer in your room. I searched everywhere and couldn't find you." After Kalen had stopped searching, he'd gone back out to the living room and stared out the glass door at the sun glinting off the pool.

Jax told him, "The tree house. We were always in the tree house. Smith too, believe it or not, but once he got that game system, it was harder to get him to go."

"Yeah, your mom told me. I found you guys out there, and you were reading Mia a story. You used different voices for each character. I was mesmerized. I mean, you were eight, and I wouldn't hire you to do voice-overs, but I was more fascinated by the book you were reading than I was in the brand new video game your brother had."

"That doesn't really answer the question."

"I look back on all the times I talked to you and watched you, and after these last two weeks, I realize we share a lot of common interests. No, we aren't the same person, but I like you just the way you are, Jax. All the rest doesn't matter."

Jax just stared at him for a minute before asking, "How long have you had a crush on me?"

Kalen smiled. "Two years, mostly. I think I had puppy love before that, but around the time you turned sixteen was when I looked at you and realized I really liked you."

Jax's eyes shuttered a bit. "Because of my looks." He started to roll away from Kalen before Kalen wrapped his arms around Jax, bringing him closer.

"No, Jax. You are good looking, there's no denying that, but you are the most beautiful person on the inside, more beautiful than anyone I know." Kalen paused trying to find a way to explain his feelings to Jax. "Yes, your looks play a part, that's just plain old attraction, but the last two weeks you showed me who you are…the whole you. I thought I liked the guy I knew when you were sixteen. But you, as you are now, are better than I could have hoped for."

"Is that why you stopped showing me affection? Because of your crush?" Jax sat up a little bit like the thought just dawned on him.

Kalen barked out a laugh. "You try crushing on your best friend's little brother at eighteen when hard-ons happen because the wind blows. It was so embarrassing, so it was just easier to stop. Plus, I didn't think you wanted my affection."

Jax smiled and relief flooded Kalen's body.

"Then this," Jax said gesturing between them, "isn't just us hooking up to you?"

Kalen brushed his fingers across Jax's cheek, wanting to soothe the fear and apprehension he could see in Jax's eyes. "This was *never* about a hook-up for me. You mean too much to me for that."

Jax pushed Kalen onto his back and crawled over his body. It was times like these, when their bodies were connected, that Kalen knew he wanted this man by his side. He wanted to sleep next to him every night, fuck him and be fucked by him. He just wanted Jax.

Kalen kissed Jax, running one hand over Jax's back and using the other to thread his fingers through Jax's hair and hold him close. He loved the taste of him, the feel of his hard body rutting against Kalen's, the sound of his moans pouring out of him.

"Shirt off." Need turned Jax's voice husky and sent tingles through Kalen's body. Jax sat back on his knees, pulling his own shirt off and giving Kalen room to sit up and remove his, tossing it to the side.

Jax shoved Kalen flat on the mattress again. He ran his hands over every inch of Kalen's chest, making his nipples tighten. Kalen let his eyes fall shut, enjoying the sensations Jax was causing in his body. Then he felt Jax's mouth on his cloth-covered cock and nearly shot off the bed.

Up on his elbows, Kalen looked down. The sight of Jax mouthing at his dick, soft hair falling in his eyes, cheeks flushed, had Kalen reaching for him. He had to touch him. Running his fingers along his shoulder, up his neck, then threading them into Jax's hair. Not to push, but to just hold on, to feel connected to Jax.

Jax moaned, the sound vibrating through Kalen's body. The heat of Jax's mouth enveloping him through his sleep pants was everything. But Kalen wanted more.

"Jax, I want you in my mouth."

Jax stopped what he was doing and looked up. His eyes wide, Jax's mouth gaped open. Kalen laughed. Sitting up, he pushed Jax's mouth closed. "Take your pants off and lay on your side. Head down there." Kalen pointed to the end of the bed.

Jax gave him a jerky nod and moved to do what Kalen said. When they were in position, Kalen was finally able to look at Jax in a way the previous things they'd done hadn't allowed. Kalen leaned in, buried his nose in Jax's balls, and took a deep breath. He moaned, not being able to stop himself. Kalen loved the scent of him there. Loved breathing it in and having it fill him up.

"God, you smell good."

Kalen ran his tongue from the base of Jax's cock to the tip. He felt the veins under his tongue, and the silk over steel of his erection, the taste of Jax filling him, making him lightheaded with want.

Jax mirrored every move Kalen made. With each lick and suck, Kalen climbed higher, each throaty growl and needy moan brought him closer to breaking apart. Kalen never thought he would need someone like he needed this man. He never thought he'd be able to get Jax to make those sounds.

Yet, he was there with Jax's cock thrusting into his mouth, his own prick wrapped in Jax's wet heat.

The sounds they were making grew louder, their breathing heavier. Kalen felt his balls draw tight and needed to warn Jax.

Pulling his mouth off Jax's cock, he said, "Fuck, I'm gonna come already."

"Me too," Jax cried out.

Kalen jerked Jax's cock, and Jax pulled off to do the same to him. "Fuck, you're so sexy. I love the way you taste. You stay just like that and keep stroking me, okay? I want you in my mouth when you come."

No sooner had Kalen wrapped his lips around Jax's dick and sucked, Jax cried out as a thick ribbon shot out of him, filling Kalen's mouth. The sound of Jax's cries had Kalen shooting a moment later.

They lay there breathless for a few moments before Kalen scooted around to face Jax. What he saw had him growling. Jax was covered in Kalen's come from his chin to his chest. Kalen leaned in and licked at Jax's chin, cleaning it all off. He pulled back and stared at the come covering Jax's chest then reached over and rubbed it into Jax's skin.

Kalen felt like he was claiming Jax as his. Afraid of what Jax would think, he avoided his eyes as he rubbed.

"I'll go get a warm cloth to clean up," Kalen said softly. But before he could move, a finger was under his chin. Jax forced Kalen to look into his eyes, and once again, Kalen couldn't breathe. Jax looked intense.

"That was so fucking hot. Next time, I get to rub *my* come into your skin." Kalen loved the sound of that.

They got cleaned up, and it was time for Kalen to go back to his bed.

"Goodnight, Jax." Kalen bent down and kissed Jax's temple.

Jax reached out before Kalen could stand, gripping his wrist. Kalen locked eyes with Jax.

"Stay. Sleep in here with me tonight?"

Kalen nodded, a lump caught in his throat, blocking any words from coming out.

Kalen lay awake for quite some time, enjoying the feel of Jax practically lying on top of him, their arms wrapped around each other.

He was so gone for this guy.

CHAPTER ELEVEN

Jax

'Little Death' Never Killed Anyone

Jax had surprised Kalen when he asked to be tied up. But after experiencing the other end and watching Kalen lose himself in the moment, Jax couldn't stop thinking about it. Kalen had been careful and asked Jax if he was sure, knowing how big a step it was for someone as inexperienced as Jax was. He wasn't wrong, but doing it with Kalen made everything feel safer, and all Jax could think about was how hot it was going to be.

Jax was on his knees, chest to the mattress. He felt his legs being spread wider, his ass tilted up, his hands cuffed together under his stomach. He tugged on the cuffs, pulling them apart—or at least trying to. He didn't want his hands to be released, but he couldn't help testing them. The knowledge that he couldn't get his hands free, that he was at Kalen's mercy even in this small way, made him hard. They'd decided that cuffing his hands together was restraining him enough…this time. Oh, and the cock ring…*Can't forget that.*

He *wanted* this.

Kalen had made sure Jax knew that if, at any time, he wanted things to stop, Jax just had to say *no*, and Kalen would stop everything.

Kalen tickled his fingers down Jax's spine. Jax thrashed, unable to handle the sensation, his nerve endings on fire. Kalen's finger circled his rim, trailed down to his balls before he reached between Jax's legs to squeeze his cock. Jax writhed and moaned. He couldn't stop himself.

The cock ring Kalen had put on him was keeping Jax so fucking hard. Even the skin there was sensitive from Kalen's hand stroking him over and over.

Kalen spread Jax's ass cheeks, and Jax shivered. Kalen was staring at his hole. It was the first time, and when Kalen spread him wide, the feeling of being exposed barreled through Jax. He was feeling this all for the first time. The idea that no one had ever touched him in this way, that it was Kalen who was the one to do it, made every touch that much hotter.

Jax felt Kalen's tongue first circle his rim then it lashed back and forth, up and down, making him tremble. He'd never known sex could be like this. Could be so powerful that it shook someone to their core.

After what felt like forever of Kalen torturing him, Kalen's tongue circled Jax's hole. God…how was he going to handle more if just Kalen's tongue could make Jax feel like the earth was shaking beneath him? Then his tongue was pushing inside, and Jax moaned and squirmed. He felt like he was on fire, like lava was flowing through his veins. It was overwhelming and not enough. It was the same feeling just being around Kalen gave him but better, more intimate.

With each thrust of Kalen's tongue, Jax just wanted more. He was pretty sure he was going to be begging Kalen to do this to him *every damn day*.

Then Jax felt it. Kalen was pushing into him with his fingers—no, just one finger. Jax had never done this to himself. He'd wanted to many times, but the idea of doing it alone had held no appeal. Now, in that moment, Jax was never more grateful he had waited.

Kalen's finger is in my ass!

"Do you need more?"

Jax nodded, unable to get words to form with how desperate he felt.

"I gotta hear you say the words, baby."

"Please, Kalen. More."

Ever so slowly, Kalen added another finger. Jax felt stretched and open.

The burning was there…Kalen had warned him that it would come. But when Kalen's hand wrapped around his cock and stroked him, everything felt…better. The pain and pleasure at the same time made Jax feel like he was floating.

How did people get anything done if they could do this all day?

Jax couldn't tell how long Kalen had fucked him with two fingers or when he had added the third, he just knew he didn't want it to end. But his body had other ideas. Jax could feel his orgasm building. He was on the brink, desperate to go over.

Kalen let go of Jax's cock at the same time he pulled his fingers out of Jax's hole. Jax felt empty, unable to comprehend what was going on. A rumble came from his chest, spilling out through his lips.

"Not yet, Jax. No yet. I want to play some more."

Again and again, Kalen licked, and finger fucked him, bringing Jax to the edge then backing off.

Jax lost count how many times Kalen had brought him to the edge.

Kalen denied him every time.

Jax sobbed and shook.

"Fuck…Kalen. I…need…more."

Jax cried out when Kalen's finger sunk into his hole again. He sunk into the bed, relaxing into the feeling of being filled by Kalen. It wasn't enough, but it was a start…for now.

"How's that?" Before Jax could respond, Kalen pulled out of him then pushed back in with two fingers. There was no burn this time, not after taking three of his fingers before. Now it felt like home and satisfaction.

"Please," Jax begged.

"I got you, Jax." Kalen licked around the fingers in Jax's hole, and Jax whined, shivers running down his spine. Jax pushed back against Kalen's fingers.

"Kalen, please—*oh fuck*…" he breathed out as Kalen speared three fingers inside him. "It's not enough. I need…need more."

Kalen paused, pulling back, then his fingers were gone, leaving Jax feeling empty. He whimpered when the bed shook, thinking Kalen was moving away for some reason. Kalen lay next to him on his side, face gentle and full of affection. He cupped Jax's cheek.

"Are you asking for me to fuck you, Jax?"

Jax took a deep breath, needing to clear some of the fog that had clouded his mind.

"Yes. I want that." Kalen opened his mouth, but with a shake of his own head, Jax stopped him. "I'm sure, Kalen. I couldn't be any *more* sure than I am right now."

Kalen searched his face, and Jax smiled, hoping to reassure him. Kalen must have found what he was looking for because he grinned and kissed Jax.

Kalen climbed off the bed, opening the bedside table drawer. He searched around a few seconds before closing the drawer and turning to face Jax.

"I have to run to my room. Stay right there, gorgeous."

Jax laughed. "Where would I go?"

Closing his eyes, Jax heard Kalen's bare feet slapping against the hardwood floors as he ran out the door and down the hall to his room. Jax giggled to himself thinking of Kalen's hard cock bouncing as he ran. It reminded him of that elephant GIF with the elephant's trunk flailing about.

"I leave you for less than a minute and you've lost your mind."

Jax popped his eyes open, seeing Kalen's smiling face a foot away where he was bent over the side of the bed, staring at Jax.

"I just thought of something funny."

"Hmm…you'll tell me later."

Jax swallowed and nodded, suddenly nervous, knowing what was happening next.

"Hey, you okay?" Kalen whispered, caressing Jax's cheek.

"Yeah, just…It's big, ya know?"

A smile pulled at Kalen's lips. "I'll take that as a compliment." Jax laughed.

"That's not what I meant, jackass."

"It'll be okay, Jax, and you can change your mind at any time."

"I know that, but I won't. I want this with you."

Kalen nodded and climbed on the bed, back behind Jax.

"But you better not have grabbed the bacon condoms," Jax teased.

"You ruin all my fun, Superstar."

Jax heard the snick of the bottle of lube right before he felt the cool liquid pouring down over his hole. Jax felt like he might shake right out of his skin in anticipation. Then came the sound of the foil packet being ripped open. He closed his eyes again, trying to imagine Kalen prepping himself—rolling the latex down his shaft, pouring lube into his hand, then stroking his hard cock to coat it.

Jax reached toward his own prick, only to feel Kalen wrapping his hand around it instead. Jax cried out.

"Don't. I'll finish," Jax groaned.

Kalen moved above him, draping his hard body over Jax's.

"Just slicking it up for you. Once I get inside you, I want you to start stroking yourself, Jax. I want to be inside you so bad. Don't be surprised if I bust the second I'm inside that tight hole."

"I'm right there with you, Kalen. I want this."

The head of Kalen's dick pushed at his rim, slowly pushing the tip inside of him. Jax tensed, not sure what to expect.

"Oh, damn, that's good," Kalen whispered right into Jax's ear.

Kalen took his time letting Jax adjust to his size and the slight pain, until he was seated completely inside Jax. Jax sighed as his body adjusted. He felt full, but the aching need caused by wanting Kalen was still there, alive and needing to be fed.

"You okay?"

"Yeah, I am. Just…fucking move please."

Kalen's chuckle was dirty. He pulled out then pushed back in, and Jax moaned. Jax grabbed his cock and stroked himself. With every push in, Jax saw stars. It was just as good as he thought it would be. Jax had never felt so connected to another person before. Just Kalen. Only ever him.

Sweat trickled down Jax's temple. Having Kalen inside of him, fucking into him, was bliss. Jax felt Kalen peppering kisses on his neck and shoulders as he thrust, taking what he wanted and giving Jax everything he needed at the same time.

Jax's hand picked up speed on his cock when he felt the warmth building at the base of his spine, the tingle in his balls as they pulled up tighter to his body. It was going too fast. He wanted to last longer, but after what had felt like hours of being teased by Kalen, he couldn't hold it back.

"Fuck yes. I'm…there."

The room spun, and Jax felt like he was coming apart at the seams.

"Yes, I'm right there with you."

Jax's orgasm hit, grabbing him and holding him tight, then shot through him like a freight train. His knees collapsed under him. Jax was sure his bones liquefied, and he was nothing but a puddle.

Kalen followed him down, his cock never leaving Jax's hole, and he shuddered, pushing deeper into Jax, staying there. The groans of ecstasy coming from Kalen were enough to get Jax's cock to twitch in envy.

Kalen fell onto him, both of them panting but Jax loving the weight of Kalen on top of him. The room smelled of sweat and sex, and Jax just wanted to breathe it in. It was them. Their scents combined, and it felt like a marking, like a symbol of them claiming each other.

"Holy shit, that was…" Kalen's husky voice made Jax shiver.

"Yeah, that was…wow." Jax laughed causing Kalen to groan.

"Don't laugh!"

Jax realized every time he laughed, his muscles tightened around Kalen's dick. It only made him laugh more, starting a chain reaction, until Kalen slowly pulled out of him.

"Jackass," Kalen grumbled.

"Your traits must be rubbing off on me," Jax replied.

"Give me ten minutes, and I can rub off on you all you like," Kalen teased, winking at him.

They both laughed again.

Kalen got up, pulling off the condom and tossing it in the trash can beside Jax's bed, as Jax rolled over onto his side, a slight wince with the movement. Kalen came back and took the cuffs off him, tossing the restraints to the end of the bed before lying back down next to Jax.

Jax's hands were finally free, so he reached out and touched Kalen. The only downside to having his hands tied up was missing this. He pulled Kalen to him, kissing him deep and hard.

"What are you thinking right now, Jax?"

"I'm thinking I want to do that again, but I'm kind of hungry."

They laughed. Jax found that he did that a lot with Kalen. He made Jax feel good. Such a simple feeling to some, but to Jax, being able to have this closeness to someone, to trust someone as much as he did Kalen, meant a lot. He'd only ever been close to his siblings, but that held no comparison to what he had with Kalen.

"Then by all means, let's go have our mid-day Thanksgiving feast and fill that bottomless pit of yours."

Quickly dressing in sleep pants and t-shirts, they walked out of Jax's room and down the hall to the kitchen.

"Why don't you go in the living room and find us something Thanksgiving-y to watch on TV, and I'll go prepare our food."

"Sure." Jax turned toward the living room and sat down on the couch. Grabbing the remote, he flicked through the channels before settling on something for them to watch.

Jax's family didn't have a lot of traditions since his parents were the adventurous type. They tried to change things up every year or left things flexible so if things like Mia's out-of-country trip came up, they could go without worrying about canceling plans with friends or relatives who were coming over. But watching the Macy's Thanksgiving Day Parade was something they tried to do no matter where they were. He bet Smith was watching it, too.

Kalen carried their food in and quickly noticed what was on the TV.

"Really? This?" Kalen shook his head and smiled, then placed their food on the coffee table.

"Yup, it's a Marsh family tradition."

Jax grabbed one of the frozen turkey meals Kalen had heated up for them off the table and started to rip off the plastic covering.

Kalen followed suit then handed Jax his fork. "I knew you Marshes were weird. How did I not know about this?"

"I don't think you've ever been over at our house for Thanksgiving, right?"

"Yeah, probably not. My mom was a stickler for that when I was living at home. Smith had come over to ours a few times, though."

The parade was playing low in the background as they ate their food. Kalen had thought it was cute when he'd seen the meals in the frozen food section before Thanksgiving. Neither one of them knew how to cook a turkey, or wanted to try, but this was the perfect substitution.

"Hey, Kalen?"

Kalen put his fork down and turned to look at Jax. "Yeah?"

"Are we…The guys are all coming home in two days."

Jax didn't know why asking this was so hard. He trusted Kalen and knew he wasn't the type to hide, but for Kalen, dating his best friend's little brother complicated things.

Jax could just ignore his brother.

"Sad, I know. Then the house will be full of loudmouths again, and I won't be able to make you scream anymore." Kalen let out a very put-upon sigh. Jax laughed and bumped his shoulder against Kalen's.

"You know that's not what I meant."

"I'm not hiding, Jax. I wouldn't do that to either one of us."

"You know that means telling Smith, right?"

Kalen groaned. "Don't remind me."

"Probably Mia, too." Jax pressed his lips together, trying to hold in his smile.

"No way. She's scarier than Smith. You can tell her." Kalen laughed.

"Such a nice boyfriend you are."

Jax stabbed a forkful of the warm brownie from Kalen's tray and shoved it into his mouth.

"Hey, stop stealing my food! And I'm the best." Kalen grinned.

"For a bacon thief," Jax teased.

They sat and ate the rest of their meal, watching and chatting about the parade. It was so easy between them. Once their food was gone, Jax leaned into the corner of the couch, Kalen leaning into him, his back pressed to Jax's chest, his head on Jax's shoulder.

Jax played with his hair as Kalen flicked through channels trying to find something else to watch.

"Hey, Kalen?" Jax said, his mouth right next to Kalen's ear.

"Yeah?"

"We can tell him together when he comes home in two days, yeah?"

"I'd love that."

Jax did, too.

CHAPTER TWELVE

Kalen
It's About Damn Time

"SMITH JUST TEXTED ME. THEY SHOULD BE HERE IN ABOUT TEN MINUTES," Jax said.

Jax and Kalen were in Jax's room, lying together. Kalen had his head on Jax's chest, resting over his heart. Listening to the beats calmed him. There was not one part of Kalen that wanted to have the upcoming conversation with Smith.

"You know he won't be mad, yeah?"

Kalen did know that. Smith just wasn't the type to get mad. He was Mr. Calm all the time. It was one of the reasons Kalen and Smith had become friends. Kalen was loud and funny, ruffling feathers the only way he knew how, and Smith was the one who smoothed the way for them and even talked them out of getting into trouble a few times.

That didn't mean Smith was going to be okay with his best friend dating his younger brother.

"Mmmhhmm."

Jax laughed softly. "You do not sound convinced."

Kalen smiled. "With good reason. Smith doesn't get mad, but he may not be happy."

They both heard the front door open at the same time and numerous voices yelling their names.

"Alright, scaredy cat, let's go face the pack of wolves."

Kalen pushed up on his arms, then straddled Jax's body. "I am no such thing. I'm the bravest person who's ever braved before." Kalen put his hands on his hips, trying to strike a superhero pose while straddling Jax's body. The laughter that came out of Jax told Kalen he'd failed.

Looking down at his boyfriend—*holy fuck, I get to call him my boyfriend*—he smiled.

"You're lucky I like you, brat." He gave Jax a quick kiss and climbed off his lap.

They went out to greet their roommates who were all still in the front hall of the house.

"Look, trouble's home," Kalen called out.

Too many back slaps and traveling horror stories later, everyone was either tucked away in their rooms or the kitchen. Kalen looked over at Jax when they were left alone, and the front of the house was back to being quiet.

"I don't think I truly understood how loud we all are until they weren't here." Kalen shook his head. "Wow."

Jax laughed. "I know. Of course, I'm used to quiet. I'm pretty sure your brain is never quiet."

"I have a wonderful brain, used for many amazing things. But yeah, none of those things are for quiet," Kalen joked.

"Let's go find my brother. I'm sure he's in his room." Jax grabbed Kalen's hand and pulled him along. Most people thought because Jax was quiet he was a pushover. If only they could see him now.

They went upstairs, and Jax stopped in front of Smith's door and looked over at Kalen, mouthing the words, "You ready?"

Kalen gave him a quick peck on the lips then nodded.

When Jax knocked on the door, Smith called out, "Come in."

Opening the door, Jax stepped in first, Kalen following behind him.

Smith was unpacking his bag, separating dirty laundry that came out of it, his TV running on low in the background. "Hey, Jax. Kalen. What brings you both to my room? Miss me already?" Smith teased.

"In your dreams, dude." Kalen was sure his voice hadn't been steady when he'd said that. And going by the confused look on Smith's face, Kalen bet he was right.

"Smith, we actually have something we need to talk to you about." Jax sat on the loveseat on the far side of the room. Kalen eyed the space next to him and decided to say *fuck it* and sit by Jax. It didn't matter how close they sat. They were telling Smith anyway.

"I'd like to introduce you to my boyfriend," Jax said, gesturing toward Kalen.

Kalen couldn't believe he'd blurted it out like that. Kalen felt a little stunned, so he couldn't imagine how Smith felt.

"What?" Smith had confusion written all over his face.

This time it was Kalen who spoke. "You had to have seen Jax and I hanging out more the weeks before break, right? We…like each other, and over break while everyone was gone, we got to know each other even better."

"A lot," added Jax.

"We're dating. To see where things go between us."

Smith stared at them, back and forth for a few moments. Then he smiled. "It's about damn time."

What?

"But…you're not upset or anything?"

"I'm pretty sure Smith knew before he left for break," Jax said. Kalen looked at Smith, his smile growing.

"Oh my god, you knew and said nothing."

Smith replied, "I couldn't say anything. It was against the rules."

"Against what rules?" Jax asked. For once, Kalen wasn't the only one in the dark in this conversation.

"The rules of the bet. Which *I* won, for the record." Smith rubbed his hands together gleefully.

"There's a bet?" Kalen yelled. "Who made the bet? What's the bet about?"

Smith laughed. "Calm down, Kalen. We've had the bet going for a while, but when things started changing between you two, we all got together and picked out dates as to when you'd hook up." Smith shrugged.

"What did you choose?" Jax asked.

"Thanksgiving."

"You owe us a cut of your prize. I cannot believe you all made a bet."

"I can," Jax replied, a smile lighting up his face.

"I'm not giving you shit, dude." Smith continued, "Besides, I've known for years you had a crush on Jax. You suck at hiding it."

Kalen wasn't known for his poker face.

"I could use the cash since the vacation nearly wiped me out," Smith said. Smith wiped the smile off his face, and he looked at them. "I'm happy for you both, honestly. I know I tease, but I see how happy Jax is, Kalen, and I know that's partly because of you." Looking over at Jax, Smith said, "Your boyfriend ain't so bad. Messy, though, so watch out for that."

It was all the blessing Kalen needed from his best friend. Smith stood and hugged them both before barreling out of the room and yelling, "Pay up, suckers! I won the bet!"

Jax laughed and Kalen sighed.

"He's such a dork," Kalen said.

"Yeah, he is," Jax replied then continued a moment later, "now we just have to tell Mia and my parents."

Kalen groaned. "I'm going into hibernation for the winter."

"It's not that bad. They already love you. One hurdle gone," Jax teased.

"How about we go to your room and make out?"

Jax laughed then stood up, grabbing Kalen's hand on the way and tugging him out of the room. Kalen watched Jax—smiling, happy—and a swell of pride filled his chest. He was a lucky guy, getting to be with him. Even luckier knowing Jax's family would already accept him, and that he got to live with Jax every day.

Kalen couldn't ever remember being this happy.

They never did get to make out in Jax's room. Instead, they spent the night with their roommates, being teased for holding hands, listening to Smith's and Dean's stories about skiing, Logan's and Reid's stories about home, and just general catching up.

It was late by the time Kalen and Jax walked into Jax's room. They seemed to always gravitate there, since Jax's bed was bigger.

Kalen stripped off his shirt as soon as they walked into the room. He was beat after the day they'd had and just wanted to get in bed and shut it all down.

Jax was watching him and started to do the same. Once they were ready for bed, they climbed in and wrapped around each other.

"I'm happy, Kalen."

"I'm glad, Superstar. I am, too." Leaning down, he kissed Jax's temple. "I've never been happier."

Kalen liked hearing that Jax was happy, knowing he had a hand in bringing some sunshine into Jax's life. He knew they'd face challenges. Just because they were together didn't mean Jax would suddenly start to like going out and being around people or Kalen would stop being sociable and stay home with Jax. It meant compromise and communication so they both would get what they needed from each other.

"What are the chances of convincing them all to go away for winter break?" Kalen asked and Jax laughed.

"You know that's not happening. They'd probably stay here just to spite us if we asked."

"Too true."

Jax turned off the lamp on his nightstand. "Goodnight, Kalen."

Kalen loved that they slept together every night. Well, except for one thing…"It will be if you stop stealing the covers."

Jax gasped. "I do not do that."

"Yes, you do. If I don't stay plastered to you, I freeze. But then sometimes you dream and flail, and I get assaulted, so I lose either way."

"You're crazy, Kalen." Jax squeezed him.

"Yeah. But I'm your crazy," Kalen replied.

"And I'm yours."

EPILOGUE

Jax
Ring Pops and Giant Peckers

KALEN HUNG THE LAST OF THE LIGHTS ON THE TREE THEY'D PUT UP IN Kalen's room the day before. There was a tree in the living room, but Jax wanted one just for them so they could give their gifts to each other. With a houseful of guys—who refused to go on another trip—it was hard to find private time and exchanging gifts for the first time at Christmas was important.

The gifts were already wrapped and under the tree, but Kalen wouldn't stop fiddling with the decorations, insisting it wasn't perfect enough yet. Jax just smiled at him, letting him go on about the lights and the position of the bulbs. But now it had been almost an hour since Kalen started, and it was getting out of hand.

"Babe, I think it's beautiful. Can we open our gifts now?"

Kalen stepped back and studied the tree. Jax thought he was being adorable. The tree only stood three feet tall and was more Charlie Brown than full Douglas fir.

His boyfriend walked over to where Jax sat on the loveseat and plopped down next to him.

"I can give you mine first," Jax said.

"You already did," Kalen said with a wink.

"So full of innuendo, even on Christmas."

Kalen handed his gift to Jax, and he did the same with Kalen's gift.

They tore at the paper, Jax much more reserved at it than Kalen. Soon the floor was littered with ripped wrapping paper. Kalen had bought a bunch of books and a few movies for Jax. He'd really put some thought into it, because a couple of the movies were ones Jax had been wanting from when he was a kid. Jax had pictures of them both they had recently taken printed and framed along with a gift card for Kalen's favorite coffee shop and one for his favorite pizza place.

They each had one more gift to open.

Exchanging wrapped boxes one last time, Jax smiled at Kalen.

"Oh, Superstar, that is an evil smile on you right now. What is in this box?"

Jax laughed. Something he was always doing, and the one thing Kalen made sure to get him to do every day.

"Let's just open them."

"Okay, I'll go first," Kalen said. Jax nodded and watched as Kalen ripped open the paper. Prying open the flaps on the box, Kalen pulled out the item inside.

As soon as Kalen held it up to get a good look, he busted out laughing. Jax grinned, loving not only that he could make him lose it like that, but also being witness to how free Kalen was.

"Oh my god, I cannot believe this." Standing up, Kalen threw the neck of the apron around his own neck then tied it around his back, and Jax lost it.

The apron had a naked torso on the front, except this one had a chest, abs, and legs…with a giant cock hanging down between its legs. When Jax had ordered it online, he'd laughed the whole time since the website called it the '*Giant Pecker Apron*.'

"Don't think I won't wear this to cook. Even if the guys are home."

"I have no doubts of your bravery."

Kalen gestured for Jax to open his. Jax tore off the paper, tossing it on the floor, and ripped the box to get what was inside. Noticing the gift itself was wrapped as well, Jax glared at his boyfriend, who did not look apologetic in the least.

Removing the last layer of paper in seconds, Jax came face to face with a ring pop. And not just any ring pop, but one that was attached to a very large butt plug.

Jax and Kalen had become a bit adventurous in their play and implemented new toys every once in a while, but Kalen just loved to give him funny or odd sex toys for fun. This one, Jax could see them using.

Jax laughed. "We're the dorks who give sex toys for Christmas."

Kalen responded, "I know, we're pretty awesome."

Jax couldn't help it. It'd been burning inside him for a couple of weeks now. It had happened so fast, he kept thinking it was too soon, but looking at Kalen's happy face he knew it was time.

"Hey, Kalen?"

"Yeah, Superstar?"

"I love you."

Kalen looked at him, his face a mask of shock and wonder. Kalen sat back down next to him, gripped his face between his hands, and kissed him. Jax felt like Kalen was pouring all of his emotions into him. He reached out and wrapped his arms around Kalen in return.

They were breathless by the time Kalen pulled back. They locked eyes, Jax watching all the emotion swirling in Kalen's eyes.

"I love you, too, Jax."

The End

ABOUT MORNINGSTAR ASHLEY

Morningstar Ashley is a transplant from New York, and now finds herself in the heartland of cowboys and longhorns—Texas. Armed with her imagination, wit, and trusty sidekicks in the form of her two crazy kids, devoted dorky husband, multiple dogs, and rambunctious cats, Morningstar spends her time reading the books she loves, crafting her own characters, and arguing the merits of hot chocolate over the bitter brew known as coffee. (Hot chocolate wins, FYI.)

After a lifetime of trying to get people to realize her first name wasn't Ashley, Morningstar decided the best way to settle the debate was to put her name on a book cover. Now she finds the accomplishment of publishing so satisfying her mind won't stop creating stories of love across the spectrum of LGBTQA+.

MORE FROM MORNINGSTAR ASHLEY

Kink Chronicles

Open Mind

Open Encounters

Open Play (Coming Soon)

A Begin Again Novel

A Different Light

Risking It All

Standalones

Letting Go

The Fates Design

The Fates Design (*Coming 2020*)